Stony Limits

For stony limits cannot hold love out:
And what love can do, that dares love attempt;
Therefore they kinsmen are no stop to me.

Shakespeare, *Romeo & Juliet*

Heartlines

Heartlines

Jane Pitt

Stony Limits

A Pan Original

First published 1985 by Pan Books Ltd,
Cavaye Place, London SW10 9PG
9 8 7 6 5 4 3 2
© Jane Pitt 1985
ISBN 0 330 28845 8
Printed in Great Britain by
Collins, Glasgow

Chapter 1

'It's cold!' Pia scowled and pulled her anorak around her. 'If this is what Nan calls an Indian summer, I'm glad Mum didn't decide to take us to India!'

'Oh, shut up and stop moaning!' Jodie was watching a tiny figure further down the valley. It wasn't Sam. She knew it wasn't Sam. He'd gone into Manchester with his father for the day to buy paint.

'Don't say anything to your mother,' he'd laughed at her. 'But I think all this is because of her! Dad's decided to do out the sitting-room. He says it's depressing him. It's been depressing him for the last five years,' he'd added thoughtfully while she'd watched him, frowning at the way she was feeling, 'but he's never bothered before.'

Jodie put her chin in her hands and tried to ignore Pia's grumbling mumbles in the background.

She'd never met anyone like Sam, and the confused, excited, upset feeling that kept threatening to choke her at the most unexpected times worried her.

'It's okay for you!' Pia was back, launching her ten-year-old self in a scramble of jeans and flying hair into a place on the dried grass. '*You're* not going to have to go to school! *You're* not going to get stuck away with all those other kids who can't even blow their noses without asking somebody's permission!

You', Pia stuck her tongue out at her sister, 'are going to be a lady of leisure until everybody makes up their minds what to do about you. But *I'm* the one who'll have to suffer!'

'You were also the one', Jodie shredded some of the grass seeds into a tiny pile in the palm of her hand, 'who thought all this was a great adventure, remember? You couldn't wait to get out of Sydney! You kept telling everybody how you were going back to the "old country" to become a "Pommie". It sounded disgusting at the time and it still does! I was perfectly happy where we were. And at least I didn't have to share a room with you, like here!'

'That's not my fault, either.' Pia pulled another face and turned on to her stomach, facing away from the valley towards the ridge. 'That's Nan's fault. In fact,' she said logically, 'if you think it through from the very beginning, it's *all* Nan's fault. And if she hadn't got ill, Mum wouldn't have got a conscience, and we wouldn't have had to come here at all.'

'Yes we would, sooner or later.' Jodie glanced at the younger girl and then frowned again. How much Pia really disliked England she couldn't be sure. At home, when she'd been growing up and stumbling round the farm in dungarees, when Dad had still been around to take care of everything, Pia had been like any other little tomboy — loud, aggressive, and an infernal nuisance.

Jodie sighed inwardly. After Dad left, Pia had changed, the same way everything had changed. She'd got even louder and more aggressive, as if his going had been something to do with all of them instead of just something between their parents.

It was a long way from New South Wales to Cheshire in England. Completely different countries; completely different lives. None of them, least of all Jodie, knew what was going to happen next.

She shivered suddenly, concentrating all her attention on the valley.

The figure had disappeared, so it really couldn't have been Sam. But something inside her had so much wanted it to be, had so much been praying that he'd got back from Manchester early – or hadn't even gone at all – that the flat empty feeling she had now made her more irritable than ever.

'Come on. Time we went back. We'll be late for tea, and you know how much Nan loves that.' She scrambled to her feet and nudged her sister with the front of her leg. 'And if you get grass stains all over those jeans, it'll only make everything a *lot* worse!'

'If Nan and Mum discover *you've* been seeing Sam Miller, you won't even live to find out what happens to me about the jeans, so stop being so big-sisterish!'

They glared at each other, then Pia broke into a giggle.

'You should see your face!' she spluttered, getting up and stretching lazily. 'You've gone white as the surf! It'll all come to a head one of these days, you mark my words.' She waggled her finger under Jodie's nose, giving a fair vocal imitation of their grandmother. 'And when it does, don't say I didn't warn you.'

'Oh shut up, *please*, Pia! You're not being funny. Just annoying. And anyway, I'm not seeing Sam Miller. Well, not in the way you mean. But the village isn't exactly huge, is it? I'm bound to bump into him occasionally, aren't I?'

'If you say so.' Pia's voice softened suddenly and she punched her sister in the arm. 'But considering we've only been here three weeks, you seem to have done a lot of bumping already. Come on. Race you to the end of the track!'

She took off, hair flying behind her, legs and arms pumping at ridiculous angles that didn't even look as if they could hold her upright.

Jodie swallowed, then looked back at the valley.

Thin wisps of smoke were hanging on the air from a dozen chimneys. The hedged fields snaked off into the distance, dotted here and there with clumps of trees and looking, for all the world, like a ridiculous patch-work quilt someone had hung out to dry from the far hills.

It was a mixture of green and pale blue haze, sparkled through with the colour of the birch and beech trees that were already dying, and a violent pang of homesickness rocked her.

On the farm, before the brief time they'd spent with their other grandparents in Sydney, there had never been this same sense of colour. Green, yes. But not this vast range of different, subtle greens. Everything had been brighter, sharper, more in focus somehow. And there had been busy sounds – from the sheep, and the birds, and the mosquitoes and horse-flies. But here, she thought fancifully, it was as if time had simply for-gotten the valley and the ridge existed. It sat in its own isolation as if nothing had touched it for centuries. And suddenly she felt some of Pia's impatience with it all. It was too quiet, too laid-back, – too, too . . . she fumbled for the thought . . . too *English*.

'Come on, possum!' Pia's voice ripped through the stillness, mocking her, laughing her back to reality, and she started to run over the short uneven turf towards the track.

'What kept you?' The younger girl was swinging carelessly on a five-bar gate. 'Suddenly catch a glimpse of Sam in the clouds?'

'Don't be a nut!' Despite herself she laughed. 'And stop going on about Sam. It only makes it worse.'

'Makes what worse?' They walked along the overgrown verge towards the village.

'Everything.' Jodie shrugged. 'I like Sam Miller. He's a nice guy. Genuine. But, well, you know. All the rest of it. With Mum. And Nan.'

She hesitated, wondering if she was making sense, even to herself. Sometimes she wished Pia was a lot older than ten. 'I can't sort of let anything else happen, can I?'

'It's your life.' Pia glanced at her, twisting the ends of her hair round her fingers. 'Nan and Mum have had theirs. They can't live yours for you. Shouldn't even try, I'd have thought. Though they probably will,' she added mysteriously.

'Yes. They will.'

'D'you really wish we hadn't left Australia, Pia?' She pulled a long dead twig from the hedgerow and examined it carefully. 'I mean, you had more friends than me there and everything, but you're younger. More adaptable, Mum says.'

'I dunno.' Pia skipped sideways to avoid two cyclists puffing up the hill towards them. 'Sometimes I think, well, it's all a laugh, all an adventure, isn't it? And it's not as if we've *got* to stay here for ever. We can go back when we're old enough if Mum decides she's not going to.

'But then I remember the farm and all the good bits, before Dad left. And that sort of makes me sniff inside sometimes. Know what I mean?'

Jodie nodded.

She'd never thought of Pia perhaps wanting to cry, and she suddenly felt guilty for all the moments when she'd shouted at her in their room in the cottage.

She'd just thought Pia was being irritating on purpose, to grab attention for herself, and hadn't considered the possibility until now that because Pia *was* only ten she was likely to be feeling even more confused and uprooted than she herself did.

'You miss Dad a lot still, don't you?' she asked, switching the top off some dead grass with the twig. 'You were always his little girl. You got on with him better than I did.'

'Yeah. Maybe. But Dad was Dad. And stop talking about him as if he's dead. Maybe we'll see him one day again as well. I overheard Mum tell Nan he's still in America. Nan just sniffed and said she always knew he'd never stay around.

Her face creased into a frown that held tears on the edge of it. 'Still, he stayed around for nearly nine years, didn't he?'

'Mmm.' Jodie nodded, trying to pull into her mind a picture of Bob Mitchenson as he'd been when she last saw him.

It had been the day before Pia's eighth birthday. They'd all been busy, Jodie fighting egg whites to make the pavlova, Mum fussing the bits and pieces together for the barbecue and Pia herself dipping her finger into the oyster soup and the various sauces.

The three of them had been laughing at Pia's nose covered in paw-paw, but the laughter had faded as the two girls had registered the expression on their mother's face.

Jodie remembered how she'd turned slowly towards the kitchen door to see her father standing there with his old canvas grip in one hand and his bush-jacket slung over his shoulder.

'You're really going then?' Her mother's voice had drifted across the heat of the kitchen, helpless-sounding and empty. 'You can't even wait until after your daughter's birthday!'

'Nope.' Their father had scratched uncomfortably at the inside of his collar, refusing to look at either of the girls. 'No point now, Karen. Decision's been made. Would've been kinder to make it years ago.

'The farm's all yours, yours and the girls'. I've seen the lawyers in Sydney. Everything's legal. Anything else you want, my folks'll take care of for you. Be better this way.'

Pia had crept towards her, scared, and she had a sudden startlingly clear picture of how they'd stood together, she with her arm around the younger girl's shoulders, neither of them understanding what was going on but both of them sensing the icy chill in the large, sunny room.

''Bye, sweetheart.' Bob Mitchenson had blown Pia a kiss from the doorway without moving. 'You make sure you take care of everybody now.'

''Bye, Karen.' He'd frowned at his wife, his sun-burned face looking craggier and more deeply etched with lines than ever before.

''Bye, Jodie. Don't be a dreamer all your life. Dream too much, you wake up one morning to discover you're dead and living's passed you by.'

'Take care.'

Then the porch screen door had clattered shut, his boots had thumped down the dusty wooden steps from the veranda, and all Jodie could remember after that had been their mother's empty sobbing scream.

'Well,' Pia suddenly pulled her out of the past by coughing explosively, 'he *did* stay around for nine years, didn't he?'

'He stayed around for fifteen,' Jodie muttered. 'You know the story anyway. How he swept Mum off her feet when he was in England, how Nan told her if she went with him she was never coming back here again . . . '

'And how Sam's dad warned her it was all going to be a terrible mistake and she'd regret it. Sam's dad loved her, didn't he?'

The hill had crested down into the beginnings of the village and the two sisters stood, looking at each other.

'Didn't he?' Pia repeated.

'Yes.' Jodie glanced away, feeling flushed and embarrassed and uneasy.

'Then maybe that's why everybody's so worried over you and Sam. Though personally I can't think what you see in him anyway! He's just another boy.'

Yes, Jodie thought again. Just another boy.

Then she took a deep breath and slowly followed Pia towards the cottage.

Chapter 2

'Where have you two *been*?' Karen Mitchenson looked at her daughters and experienced a terrible sinking feeling that had nothing to do with the fact that Pia's once-clean jeans were bright green at the knees.

It had, on the other hand, everything to do with Jodie's withdrawn expression and the light purple shadows under her eyes.

Uprooting Pia had been simple. Tell her there was an adventure and Pia would promptly go all-out to find it, attacking it in a strangely, solidly sensible fashion that was odd in a ten-year-old.

Uprooting Jodie had been something else again, and for the first time in eighteen years Karen wished she could break down, put her head in her own mother's lap, and cry.

Somehow she'd coped since Bob left. Somehow she'd managed, even with his parents, to keep the three of them together and concentrate on making the girls laugh and accept their new situation instead of tucking herself away in a corner and brooding, which was what she'd honestly felt like.

Sometimes, though, she wondered how much of her own confusion of feeling Jodie guessed at.

The girl was sixteen. A grown-up, very positive sixteen in some ways, certainly. But it was muddle enough being that age at any time. And internally it had to be even more of a muddle suddenly finding yourself in a strange country with strange customs and surrounded by strangers.

'Well?' The word shot out with more annoyance and irritability attached to it than Karen had intended. 'You know Nan has tea at half-past five. This isn't Australia now. You can't just do what you like. Or hadn't you realised that?'

'And tea is on the table.' Barbara Wright hobbled into the room, leaning heavily on the stick she had to use since she'd slipped on the icy pavements in last winter's dreadful snowstorm and broken her hip. 'It's getting cold, and I do prefer toasted teacakes to be warm, at the very least.'

Her eyes swept them both, not missing the expression of disgust on Pia's face at the mention of 'teacakes'. Presumably the child was used to chewing on raw water melon or something for Australian tea, if they ever had such a meal. Well, she'd simply have to realise that this was Britain, and Britain had certain tastes and standards which were nothing whatsoever to do with the Commonwealth. After all, if it hadn't been for the British and Captain Cook, the entire place probably wouldn't have existed.

Jodie, by contrast, was shuffling from foot to foot; she strongly reminded her grandmother of one of those stick insects she'd found on the conservatory wall last week.

It had been long and gangly, too, and when she'd put it in the glass jar with the dead twigs she'd almost imagined it had shuffled its ridiculously spindly legs and sighed — very much the way Jodie was sighing now.

She sighed herself and turned to look at Pia.

The child was a mess. Her hair needed cutting or perming at the very least. Not that she approved of perming children's hair, but Pia's was completely out of control. Her jeans were filthy, and that ancient red anorak simply had to be replaced. A shopping trip to Manchester, she felt, was called for in the very near future.

'Well?' she heard Karen say again, more softly this time.

The girls moved their shoulders back to a form of attention, and for both Barbara Wright and Karen Mitchenson, a strong sense of having been here before quivered through the room.

Barbara had often asked defeating questions like that, and Karen had always stood at the same kind of defiant attention.

'Never mind all that now,' she heard herself say testily. 'Come along, Karen. Take them through to the dining-room. I'll fetch some hot water.'

Pia giggled, and Karen shot her a filthy look. It was bad enough having to cope with being back with her mother after all these years. But it wasn't made any easier when her younger daughter had miniature fits of hysterics over the daily afternoon-tea ceremony.

She sighed aloud. She would have to talk to them both seriously because as far as she could see, now she'd actually made the step back to England, it was very probable that she – and they – would spend the next few years sharing the cottage with Barbara.

For a start she couldn't begin to think in terms of buying anywhere of her own, and she'd already explained that to them.

She'd sold the farm at a loss; her in-laws kept telling her that. After all the legalities had been tied up, after the two years in Sydney taking part-time work wherever and whenever she could get it, what money there had been had dwindled fast, and when she'd finally made the decision to come back to Britain, the three air fares had eaten into a large slice of the remainder. What was left would be needed for Pia's schooling, and to help Jodie in whatever she chose to do.

'Perhaps we shouldn't have come,' she thought wearily, sitting down at the neatly laid table with its starched and hand-embroidered cloth. 'Perhaps I should've stuck it out, tried to buy another small farm somewhere, even married again — if anybody ever asked me!'

But at the time none of these had seemed the proper answer, and the slightly rambling, complaining letters from her own mother had finally forced a slight feeling of nostalgia and homesickness into a decision.

If only, she thought, frowning at Jodie who was busy wiping butter from the teacakes off her chin with the back of her hand, Mum had at least warned me that Gordon was still living in the village! And if only she'd managed to bring herself at least to mention that he had a son called Sam who was seventeen!

She looked at Jodie again, wondering how she was really going to manage her over the next few years.

Bob had always thought Jodie was a dreamer, not a do-er. But Jodie had inherited a very stubborn streak from him, and Karen had a sneaking suspicion it was going to come to the fore in all its glory in the not too distant future.

She knew the girl had been meeting Sam Miller occasionally. The village was far too small for her not to know. There were still too many older people around who remembered her and obviously were intrigued by what her children did. But she also suspected, with a rather cold, hollow feeling, that for the first time Jodie was showing a serious and real interest in the opposite sex.

She hadn't any objections to that. It had to happen.

What she did object to was that Jodie's first falling in love was probably going to be with the son of the man who'd warned her, so firmly and so accurately as it turned out, about the unreliability of Jodie's own father.

'It's extremely quiet in here. What's the matter? Cat got your tongues?' Barbara Wright put the silver hot-water jug carefully on to its place-mat.

'Cats don't go for tongues!' Pia muttered scornfully, pushing currants from the teacakes round the plate. 'Cats go for eyes. But that's only when they feel they're being attacked. I know. We had cats on the farm. *Proper* cats,' she added scornfully, and this time it was Jodie who shot her a warning look.

'Well, they were proper.' She ignored the eye-message. 'They looked after themselves and hunted and things. They didn't just lie in the sun like Edward all day. He never does *anything*.'

'Edward's old, Pia. How old is he by the way, Mum?' Karen found herself talking too quickly and too loudly,

'You ought to know.' Her mother glared at her. 'He was a kitten when you ran off eighteen years ago.'

'Oh Mum!' Karen sighed, wishing no one had

brought up the subject of cats. 'I didn't run off, not the way you mean, and you know it. I got married to an Australian and moved to Australia. What's wrong with that?'

'Everything you left behind you here, so answer the question yourself!' Barbara Wright snapped, pouring tea into the neat bone-china cups. 'And sit up straight, Jodie. You'll be round-shouldered by the time you're twenty at this rate.'

'I – I don't think I want any tea Nan, if you don't mind. I've got a headache. It must've been the wind out on the ridge. I'd like to go and lie down, if that's all right?'

Three sets of eyes watched her as she moved the chair carefully away from the table. But for once, Barbara held her tongue.

The girl looked tired and far too pale, as if she really *did* have a headache.

She'd looked tired and pale since they'd all arrived. Listless, really, as if she'd lost all sense of purpose. She'd spent days over the first two weeks curled up on the window seat in the lounge, scratching an uncomplaining Edward between the ears and staring out at the late summer garden.

Then one day she'd announced she was going for a walk by herself, hadn't even allowed Pia to go with her, and when she'd come back her eyes had had an unnatural sparkle, as if they'd spent a lot of time crying.

Barbara could remember Karen's eyes at the same age with that same kind of sparkle, usually after some silly argument where both of them had firmly believed they were in the right.

And she could remember, much too clearly, how Karen had reacted over tea all those years ago when she, Barbara, had accused her of simply flirting with Gordon Miller.

'I'm *not* flirting!' The words echoed down from that vanished afternoon. 'I like Gordon. A lot. But I'm not in love with him, Mum! Maybe I could be. I don't know. But he's too – too quiet, somehow. I want a bit of excitement out of life.

'Now, if you don't mind, I – I don't think I want any tea. I've a bit of a headache. The wind on the ridge was pretty strong. I'd like to go and lie down, if you don't mind?'

Barbara looked across at her daughter, wondering if what Jodie had just said had brought back the same memory, but Karen was busy stacking the unused plates and cutlery neatly together on to the wooden tray.

'Can I go, too, please?' Pia bounced up. 'I've finished, and if I eat any more, I won't have room for my supper.

'What *is* for supper anyway, Nan?' She swung a dazzling smile on her grandmother. 'Have you made a steak pie? You promised you would,' she wheedled, and despite herself Barbara softened.

'Egg and bacon. *Traditional* egg and bacon,' she almost smiled. 'And a bit of salad. You can help yourselves. I'm going out.'

Karen glanced at her in surprise.

'Once a month I visit old Mrs Raffald. I've had to put it off since you've been here, but I rang her to tell her tonight would be all right.

'You'll manage on your own, won't you?' she added frostily.

'*Of course* I'll manage, Mum!' Karen laughed, hoping the relief she felt at an evening on her own didn't show in her voice, and noticing, from the corner of her eye, Pia beginning to giggle again. 'I've managed for eighteen years, haven't I?'

'That', mother and daughter faced each other, 'is entirely a matter of opinion.'

'Now Jodie, Pia, please don't stand in the doorway like knotless threads. You make the place look untidy. If you're going to your room, go.'

'Yes, Nan.' Jodie's voice was very soft. 'And I'm sorry about tea.'

Then clumsily, as if she couldn't see particularly well, the girl swung out into the hall.

'Karen?' As Pia followed her they could both hear their grandmother's voice sounding suddenly old. 'What on earth's the matter with that child? Is she lonely? Hasn't she tried to make friends in the village? Pia seems to manage.'

'Pia's Pia.' Karen Mitchenson sounded tired. 'She seems to manage anywhere. And yes, I think Jodie *has* made a friend. I think that's part of the problem.'

'Oh.' Teacups clanked on to the tray and Pia frowned at her sister worriedly, watching her as they listened. 'What kind of problem?'

'I think she's met Sam Miller. In fact, I don't *think* she has, I know she has. But what worries me, Mum,' there was the sound of the connecting door to the kitchen being opened, 'is how *often* she's met him, because there is absolutely no way I'd want her to get involved with that family. It could lead to disaster.'

'For once', Barbara's voice was indistinct over the noise of the sink filling with water and the girls had to strain to hear, 'I agree with you. It's high time you had a little chat with them, Karen. We don't want history repeating itself, do we?'

Pia closed the door quickly and quietly, crossed to Jodie and gripped her sister's arm tightly.

'Stop shaking!' she hissed. 'Nan's on her high horse and Mum's tired, that's all. They can't really stop you seeing Sam, and even if they did,' she frowned then chewed her bottom lip, 'it wouldn't be the end of the world, would it?'

'I don't expect so.' Jodie's voice came out strangled from somewhere deep in her throat. 'But you wouldn't understand, anyway, would you? You're too young. So just leave me alone!'

Then she turned and raced up the narrow staircase towards their shared room.

Seconds later Pia heard its door slam – at almost the same time as the ancient bell on the front door began to buzz.

Chapter 3

Pia hesitated, then slowly walked down the hall.

The shape on the other side of the frosted glass panel *could* have been anyone, but she had a sneaking suspicion, just from the way it was standing, that she already knew who it really was.

'Hi, Pia!' Sam Miller grinned at her nervously as she opened the door. 'I was beginning to wonder if you were all out.'

'Good day, Sam.' She swallowed hard. According to the conversation in the kitchen, he was the last person on earth who should have come knocking.

Nan was quite likely to kill him with her stick, and if Mum knew he was here she'd probably lend a hand, and then barbecue him on it.

'We're all home.' She slipped through the half-open gap and closed the door softly behind her. 'But I don't think I should ask you in. Did you want to see Jodie? She's upstairs with a headache. At least, that's what she's calling it.'

'Oh.' Sam frowned and stared down at the broken concrete path. 'Well, I suppose I was wondering if she was around, but actually Dad sent me over with this for your mum.' He fumbled in his pocket and pulled out a battered envelope. 'Maybe you'd give it to her?'

'Who is it, Pia?' Karen Mitchenson's voice made them both jump guiltily and Pia glanced behind her.

'Nobody, Mum! Well that is, actually, something for you.' She grabbed the envelope from Sam and was about to head back inside when the door was pulled fully open.

'I asked . . .' Karen stopped, looking from Pia to Sam, her face hardening.

'Hello, Mrs Mitchenson.' Sam smiled uneasily. He'd only met her once before and then he hadn't been introduced. 'Dad sent me over with a note for you. Pia's got it.' He nodded towards the envelope. 'Sorry to

22

have disturbed you.' Then with a peculiar half-bob of his head, very aware that his neck and ears had flushed scarlet, he hurried back down the path.

If he'd looked up, he'd have seen Jodie's face at the attic bedroom window. But he didn't. His only concern was to put as much distance as he could between himself and Barbara Wright's cottage.

He didn't know the full story of what had happened between his father and Jodie's mother all those years ago. He simply sensed that since Karen Mitchenson and the two girls had moved to the village his dad had become more withdrawn than ever. He spent what seemed to be endless hours in his studio-workshop, not actually working but – whenever Sam went in – sitting staring into space surrounded by old photographs of Karen and more recent ones, pinned to the walls, of Claire, Sam's own mother.

He'd tried to ask a couple of days ago, one evening after he'd got back from showing Jodie the old fenced-off mines on Alderley Edge, so he could find out what was was wrong, but Gordon Miller had simply grunted at him.

'Nothing's *wrong*, Sam.' He'd shut the photograph album he'd been holding with a slap and pushed it to one side on the cluttered work-bench. 'Just a lot of old memories raising their heads. Some of them bad. Some of them,' he'd turned to smile at his son, 'good. And some of them very sad indeed.

'Where've you been, anyway?' He'd changed the subject abruptly. 'It's late. The sun's well down.'

'I . . .' for the first time since he could remember Sam had felt reluctant to tell his father what he'd been doing. 'I just took Jodie Mitchenson for a walk. That's

OK, isn't it?'

The silence between the two of them had stretched, like the shadows in the workshop, until eventually Gordon had sighed.

'Anybody else – of course it would be all right. I trust you. Jodie Mitchenson, well, you could find a lot of problems there.

'It's not,' he'd held up his hand as Sam had tried to interrupt, 'that I know the girl, or that she isn't nice enough. But be careful, Sam. Don't get involved. I did once, and it hurt like hell!'

Then he'd got up abruptly, begun to tidy away his tools, and the conversation had been closed.

Half-way up the winding hill, towards the house he shared with his father, Sam stopped, gasping for breath and realising he'd been running hard. His lungs felt tight, and the muscles at the back of his legs felt hot and weak.

A light evening wind rustled the birches, sending the dead leaves scurrying in what looked like premature snowfalls into the ditches, and bringing with it a chill that Sam sensed meant an early frost.

He stood for a second smelling all the familiar wood smells, and wondered why he felt depressed.

From the moment he'd first bumped into Jodie in the local all-purpose, anything-from-a-fish-finger-to-a-pair-of-tights-and-a-postcard shop, he'd liked her.

She was different from the local girls. Taller, to begin with, and much thinner.

One day people would probably start calling that thinness 'slenderness', he thought, but at the moment she looked like a young tree that could well snap if the wind caught it too strongly from the wrong direction.

Her hair was mouse-blonde and very long. Sometimes he'd found himself just wanting to run his fingers through it and bury his face in it. When she walked or tossed her head, it swept out behind her like a sudden unexpected swirl of summer mist.

But her eyes — he started jogging again — they were the things about her that would always make her stand out from any crowd for him.

They were large, and an extraordinary shade of squirrel grey-brown. He'd begun to learn already that you could tell how she felt by the way her eyes looked at that moment.

Happy and relaxed and they were like drifting wood smoke. Annoyed and upset, they changed to the colour of wet dead bracken. Angry? Well, he hadn't seen her angry yet, but he could imagine how the brown shades would disappear and the grey harden and sparkle like stone in sunlight.

'Sam Miller,' he took a deep breath and slowed himself to a walk, 'Jodie Mitchenson is just a girl! She isn't poetry in motion, or a love song you've heard on the radio, or anything soppy like that.

'You only met her three weeks ago. You've only seen her a few times, and only once without that sister of hers. Stop behaving like a wally!'

But as he snatched impatiently at some old man's beard from the tangled hedge, he couldn't seem to help himself. He couldn't get her out of his mind. And two days ago, on the Edge, he'd found himself wanting to put his arms round her and kiss her.

He'd kissed girls before. Of course he had. He'd been dating casually on and off since he was fourteen. Last year he'd even firmly imagined that he was in love with

Vicky Dryden from Stockport, until one day he'd watched her laughing too loudly and showing too much of her bony chest in its tight t-shirt.

He'd gone off her there and then. Told her he'd see her around sometime and walked away, leaving her with the rest of the crowd that he really didn't go on much anyway.

Since then, there hadn't been anyone else. He'd been perfectly happy to leave school in the summer and just bum around.

Gordon hadn't pressured him about the future. There had been plenty of part-time work and odd jobs, from painting people's windows to learning the knack of repairing dry-stone walls and wooden fences. Most of it had been outdoors, and he'd enjoyed that. But he knew his dad well enough to realise that Gordon was beginning to twitch about where he went from here.

'And where *do* I go?' He said the words aloud, grinning as the startled wood pigeon who'd heard him took off in a stumbling, muttering flight from the pine trees scattered through the birches.

It was a big world outside. One full of opportunities, or so he kept hearing. But for someone who didn't really want to *do* anything, who was perfectly content to live on a day-to-day basis taking whatever came along, he had the feeling that the opportunities might not be as wonderful as they were cracked up to be.

He'd tried to explain that to Jodie, and she'd seemed to understand.

'I'm not like Dad,' he'd said. 'I haven't got a trade or profession or whatever it is you'd call Dad's work. He can make things with his hands and he enjoys it. He sells what he makes, as well, so in term time he only has to lecture two days a week.'

'Lecture?' The wind on the Edge had been blowing Jodie's hair round her face and she'd pushed it away with her hands — very long, slim hands he'd noticed — and peered at him, the sun and the dust making her wrinkle her face.

'Yes. Property law of all things! That's what he was trained in. I must've been about seven when he started to give up teaching full time. I can remember him and Mum arguing because she was the one who didn't think he should carry on with it.' He'd trailed off at that memory, and all the other memories of his mother that had suddenly crashed back.

Claire Miller had been dead for five years, but it still hurt to think about her.

'So what happened?' Jodie had moved closer to him and he hadn't been sure whether it was because she'd sensed the rush of feeling that had gone through him, or because she hadn't been properly able to hear what he'd been saying.

'Well, Dad had always played about with bits of stone and wood and things, carving them into shapes. He'd sold some to the shops in Wilmslow and Alderley, places like that, but he never thought he was good enough to do it full-time.

'One day Mum got so angry she took the car and a whole load of his stuff — and when she came back she'd sold the lot for him!' He'd laughed. 'He didn't know whether to be upset or delighted, but in the end he gave in and told her he'd try things her way.

'They were pretty happy together after that,' he'd added thoughtfully. 'Until she got ill, anyway.'

'I'm sorry,' she'd said quietly, and he shivered suddenly as he remembered the touch of her hand on his arm and the way her face had frowned compassion at him. 'I didn't realise . . .'

'Oh, it's OK. I was only ten. I didn't realise what was going on when it all started,' he'd lied, because although he hadn't understood, he *had* realised.

First there had been the hospitals and the operations, then the radiation therapy, then the diets, then the chemo-therapy. In between each section, Claire Miller had almost bubbled back to her normal self. But each time, when the treatment didn't quite work, when she'd started to lose weight and her skin had begun to take on an almost translucent yellowish glow, Sam had watched her, feeling the full impact of fear in his stomach.

He'd never talked to anyone, not even his father, about it.

Yet he'd talked to Jodie.

He climbed the gate into the overgrown orchard at the bottom of the garden and stood for a second, watching the evening sky darken with sudden storm clouds.

He'd told Jodie that, finally, when Gordon had explained that his mother was dead, he'd simply walked out of the house and disappeared for three days.

'Where did you go?' Her eyes had been larger than normal and her hand had stayed gripping his arm.

'Mow Cop,' he'd shrugged. 'It's a ruined tower on top of a hill not far from here, a really weird place. It was built in the 1750s or something, God knows why. But I wanted to be on my own. I wanted to think. Not that', he'd covered her hand shyly with his own, 'I knew what I was thinking about very much. If I had done I'd have realised I was driving Dad round the bend, running away like that.'

'How old were you by then?' The strange, slightly harsh lilt of her Australian accent had whispered round him.

'Twelve. Nearly thirteen. Why?'

'I was fourteen when my dad left. He didn't die. He just left. He told me', she'd sounded bitter, 'not to be a dreamer all my life. That if I did I'd wake up one morning to discover I was dead and life had passed me by.'

'What did you do? After he went, I mean?' He'd got to his feet and pulled her gently to hers. Then, as naturally as it it had always been happening, he'd slipped his arm round her shoulders.

'I was making pavlova. That's a sort of Australian pudding with meringue and fruit and stuff. I'd just beaten up the egg whites so they were stiff, but the heat had made them go all soggy again while Dad was doing his speech to us. They weren't any use. So I threw the bowl across the kitchen. It crashed into the porch screen and everything splattered everywhere.

'Mum laughed, but Pia started to cry, so I went out and just walked around.

'I didn't stay away three days, though,' she'd added shyly. 'I couldn't. I had to start proving I wasn't just a dreamer, like he thought.'

They'd looked at each other, smiling, and that had been the moment Sam had wanted to pull her to him and kiss her.

She was slightly taller than he was, but when she hunched herself forward against the wind, she looked like a bird who'd forgotten how to fly.

'Jodie Mitchenson,' he muttered to himself, trekking up the path towards the house.

His father had obviously finished in the workshop for the day because a light gleamed at the kitchen window and he could see a shadow moving around, busily filling the kettle.

'Jodie Mitchenson, who *are* you? Why are you doing this to me?'

As if the house had heard, the back door was suddenly flung open and he saw his dad standing there, still holding the kettle in one hand and its lid in the other.

'Sam?' he called into the gathered darkness. 'Sam, is that you? Can you come in, please? Now. I want to have a talk to you.'

Sam squared his shoulders, then moved towards the light.

It was only when he walked into the untidy kitchen that he realised Karen Mitchenson was sitting there, hand holding wrist, waiting.

Chapter 4

'Sit down, Sam.' Gordon turned his back and went to plug in the kettle.

'What's the matter? What's happened?' He looked from one adult face to the other.

His dad seemed nervous and tense, and Mrs

Mitchenson looked old and tired.

'Have I done something wrong?' He settled himself uneasily on the edge of his mother's rocking chair.

'Not as far as we know. At least,' the kettle came to an over-filled hissing boil and Gordon poured hot water into the instant coffee in three mugs, 'not yet. It's just that I feel, well, *we* feel,' he glanced at Karen Mitchenson who nodded coolly, 'that it would be better for everybody concerned if you weren't to see Jodie any more.' He handed Sam his mug and carried the other one carefully across to the woman in the straight-backed wicker chair.

Sam stared at them both, not really believing what he'd just heard.

'But why?' he stuttered, putting his mug down on the floor, certain that if he didn't he'd spill its contents everywhere and make an idiot of himself.

'Because we'd prefer it that way.' Karen's Australian accent still had an English edge to it. 'It's not that I've anything against you or', she hesitated and glanced up at Gordon, whose turn it was to nod back, 'that your father has anything against Jodie. It's simply that neither of us feels it would be advisable for you both to risk getting into any kind of relationship.'

'*Relationship*!' Sam felt himself explode. 'What're you talking about? Jodie and I are just friends! We like each other, that's all, but we hardly know each other! We're not about to run away together or something!'

'I know. I know. Now calm down.' His father frowned at him. 'But we're older and more experienced than you are, and we've both been through things that we'd prefer you and Jodie not to repeat, even by accident.'

'Sam,' Karen's voice had softened as she'd seen the confusion in the boy's face, 'your father and I had a – well, a relationship,' she stressed the last word, 'years ago. It didn't work out, for either of us. We don't want you and Jodie to be hurt the same way.'

He looked at them, then got slowly to his feet, not trusting himself to speak.

What had happened in their dim and distant pasts was their business. But he and Jodie were entirely different people! It was up to them to decide their own futures, and if these futures in any way involved each other, then that was how it should be allowed to be!

He turned and walked stiffly towards the door, hearing Karen's sharp intake of breath and sensing that Gordon had just put his hand on her shoulder to stop her saying anything more.

Everything in the kitchen seemed to have blurred, and the only sound Sam could hear was the ticking of the old grandfather clock in the corner.

He fumbled blindly for the doorknob, wondering if he was going to shout and punch something, or simply burst into tears.

'We mean it, Sam.' His dad sounded sterner than he could ever remember. 'You're not to see her again. I trust you to do what I'm asking, because I *am* asking. But if you don't, then I'll have no hesitation in sending you off to technical college in London or somewhere. You're still my responsibility until you're eighteen, and that's not for a month or two yet.'

Sam didn't wait to hear any more. He pushed open the door and fled through it to the safety of his own room.

All his life his father had been reasonable with him

and had talked to him as if they were equals. Now, he felt like a naughty child.

'I'm sorry, Gordon,' Karen said softly as the door slammed shut behind him. 'But it's for the best. Jodie's too young and impressionable. She's had a hurt time over the last couple of years. I want her to find her feet and adapt. I want her to make a lot of new friends here who'll take her out of herself and put a bit of sparkle back into her face.'

'Strangely enough,' Gordon's voice was cold, 'I want the same thing for Sam, Karen. I don't want him to suffer the way I suffered after you rushed out of my life.

'When his mother died,' he sat down drearily in Claire's chair and put his head in his hands, 'he stopped being a normal boy and hid away inside himself. He's still doing that to a certain extent, and the one thing he doesn't need is an involvement he can't handle.'

'Then we're agreed?' Karen murmured icily, getting to her feet and picking up her handbag.

She swept across the room to the back door, her high heels clicking angrily against the flagstones.

'If I'd known you were still living here and had a son just a little older than Jodie, I doubt I'd have come back to the village. In fact,' she paused with her hand on the wrought-iron latch, 'I doubt if I'd have come to England at all. Goodnight, Gordon.'

Then she let herself out into the darkness and strode towards the back gate, swallowing back tears and memories.

'Thank God,' she thought as she stumbled down the lane towards the village, wishing she'd worn more sensible shoes, 'Mum's out for the evening. Because right at this moment, facing Jodie's going to be bad enough. Facing her with her grandmother skulking in a corner downstairs listening to every word through the thin walls would be downright impossible!'

She walked tiredly up the path towards the cottage, then paused and looked back the way she'd come.

It was all such a long time ago and she'd been young and extremely foolish. She'd known Gordon had cared about her, probably cared about her far too much, and in her own way she'd been fond of him.

Maybe even, she admitted, a good deal *more* than fond. But when Bob had come along with his swash-buckling smile and general air of not wanting to stand still for even thirty seconds, she'd allowed herself to be swept so completely off her feet that neither Gordon's nor her mother's arguments and pleas for her to take a more sensible look at the situation had penetrated the shiny, excited haze of being in love for the first time.

'But it wasn't exactly a love that lasted very long,' she sighed, unlocking the cottage door and relaxing slightly in the rush of warmth from the central heating.

It might only be October, but the nights and mornings were bitterly cold by her Australian standards.

'Hello, Mum!' Pia looked up from her place in front of the television, where she was watching some pop programme with a lot of dancers gyrating around. 'Have a nice walk?'

'Very, thank you.' She slipped off her jacket and held her hands to the welcome blaze from the log fire. 'Where's Jodie?'

'Upstairs. She said she wasn't feeling very well, so she's gone to bed early. I think it's her time of the month or something. She asked me to tell you not to bother with supper for her because she still isn't hungry, and she thinks she'll go to sleep.' Pia crossed hidden fingers at the last lie.

Jodie hadn't asked her to say anything of the kind. Jodie had simply yelled at her to get out and leave her alone again, because she wanted to think, and Pia had a pretty fair idea who it was she wanted to think about.

She also had a pretty fair idea of where their mother had gone, and she sensed a blockbuster of a row hovering, particularly as Nan was out for the evening.

'Shall I get supper on trays for just us through here? You know, the way we used to sometimes at the farm?' She scrambled to her feet. 'Nan's left everything out,' and she winked mischievously, 'I just *happen* to know there's some whisky in the house! I found it at the back of the sideboard while I was rummaging. I could get you one if you like?'

Despite herself Karen laughed and gave the girl a quick hug.

'I'd like very much!' She eased off her shoes and sank down into the sofa. 'But what were you doing rummaging in cupboards?'

'Nothing,' Pia grinned innocently. 'I just like looking around, that's all! Hang on. I won't be a second!' Then she scampered out through the lounge door, closed it behind her, and skidded to a partial halt as she saw Jodie coming down the stairs.

'Go back!' she hissed, jumping from foot to foot and waving frantically.

'What?' Jodie frowned, pulling her short cotton dressing-gown closer.

'Mum's in and she looks like war's broken out! I've told her you're asleep because she's got that "little chat" expression on her face, and I didn't think you'd want one of those! Go on! Clear out!'

'Oh.' For a second Jodie hesitated, then she shot her sister a weak grin, whispered, 'Thanks!' and turned and padded back the way she'd come, praying the loose step three down from the top wouldn't squeak as loudly as it normally did.

She closed the bedroom door quietly behind her and sat on the edge of her bed, wishing the butterflies inside her stomach would stop performing circus acts.

She'd heard her mother go out and had almost broken her neck craning round the window trying to see which direction she'd taken, but she'd been almost positive it would be towards Gordon Miller's house.

'Only, why?' she asked aloud, then flung herself face down on the bed.

Pia had told her Sam had brought a letter for her mother from his father. 'And Mum looked none too pleased when she read it,' the younger girl had announced. 'She tore it up into little bits and lit the lounge fire with it. Then she went into the bathroom, slapped on her make-up and told me to double-lock the door behind her when she'd gone. She was wearing her best shoes, too.

'What's happening, Jodie?' Pia had suddenly stopped looking grown-up and sensible and gone back to being a normal ten-year-old. 'What's going on?'

'I don't know.' Jodie had turned miserably away from the window wishing Sam — when he'd left — had looked up and seen her waving at him.

'And I still don't!' she muttered into her pillow. 'All I'm certain about is that I want to see Sam Miller again, and again, and again!'

She thought back to two nights ago when they'd walked along Alderley Edge.

When he'd been telling her about his mother and about running away for three days his eyes had been so sad and his body so tense that she'd simply wanted to reach out and put her arms round him.

She'd never met anyone like him before.

All the boys back in Australia, all the beach crowd she'd known in Sydney for the last couple of years, had been brash and noisy and self-confident. For most of them, girls were a giggle, a bit of a challenge, someone to date a few times and then drop for someone else with no explanations given and only a quick 'See you!' as a goodbye.

Maybe English boys were exactly the same, but Sam seemed different.

She felt comfortable when she was with him. They didn't have to rap all the time, and on the walk along the Edge, as he called it, she'd honestly begun to feel as if she'd known him for ever.

But there was something more than all that, too. Something to do with a bubbling excitement that started deep down inside her when she saw him, and that rushed into her throat so she almost couldn't speak when they were actually close together.

She shut her eyes tightly, screwing up her face and gripping the pillow until her hands hurt.

She'd been kissed before, of course she had! At beach parties and barbecues, although she'd never particularly enjoyed the experience.

She'd even gone through a little gentle petting with Ted Hughes, who'd dated her for almost three months before he'd gone off with snobby Sally Talman from

Eastern Suburbs because her dad had given her a brand new sedan for her birthday. But none of it had really meant much, and she'd only ever gone along as far as she had because it was what everybody else seemed to be doing.

Now she rolled over on to her side, feeling suddenly hot and flushed. More than anything she wanted Sam Miller to kiss her.

She touched her midriff under the cotton housecoat and sighed.

She wanted to feel his arms round her tightly. Wanted to run her fingers through his crazy brown hair that kept falling over his face. Wanted to feel his body against hers and find out how he tasted when their lips met.

She groaned and sat up. What Pia had said that afternoon about how Nan and Mum would react if they knew she was seeing Sam – or even guessed how much she *wanted* to see him – was probably right. They'd flip, but for what real reason she couldn't begin to understand.

If something had happened between her Mum and Sam's father years ago, then that was up to them. If it had been a bad scene, then that was sad. But it didn't mean that if she and Sam got together exactly the same *kind* of things would happen, did it?

She swung herself off the bed and crossed to the window, leaning her head against the cool glass and wishing it would stop aching. That was one of the punishments you got for telling lies – eventually the lie caught up with you and turned into a reality.

'Oh Sam!' she gulped miserably, tracing his name in the misted-up patch her breath had left. '*Why* am I feeling like this?'

Then the overhead light was suddenly switched on, and she turned guiltily to face her mother.

Chapter 5

Karen looked at her daughter and inwardly sighed. The girl had a guilty restlessness about her, and she could see the word 'Sam' carefully printed on the misty window with a rather uncertain heart drawn round it.

'Hi, Mum!' Jodie was trying desperately to smile. 'Did you have a good walk? I saw you go out, but my head's still hurting and I really don't want anything to eat, which is why I stayed up here. I thought I'd maybe grab some sleep.' The words were falling over themselves, slightly too high-pitched and breathless.

Karen tried to smile herself, hoped she'd succeeded and realised helplessly she hadn't. Although her face would be twisted into its normal expression, Jodie knew her well enough to recognise that the smile hadn't properly reached her eyes.

'Sit down, honey,' she said quietly. 'We've got to have a chat.'

'Oh Mum!' Jodie swung away from the window, managing to obliterate the name and the heart with the back of her hand so the glass streaked and small droplets of water chased each other down the sill. 'Not the birds and the bees again! I know all about them, remember?'

'I do indeed.' This time Karen felt, despite herself, a true smile touch her eyes. Sometimes she wondered how she and Bob had managed to produce two such entirely different young animals as Jodie and Pia.

'I would imagine, in fact,' she settled herself into the old pink basket chair she could remember from her own childhood, 'you're much more up-to-date on these matters than I am.'

They looked at each other stiffly, neither knowing how to continue the conversation.

'Well, what else d'you want to talk about?' Jodie had crossed to the dressing-table and was fiddling with her hair, plaiting and re-plaiting thin strands on either side of her face so they hung down limply and made her look like a sad rag-doll.

'Sam Miller.' Karen watched the girl's back stiffen, watched her long slim hands flutter nervously like agitated birds.

'What about him?' Her voice was gruff and rebellious. 'He's nice. Different. I like him.' She turned and face her mother defiantly. 'A lot,' she added.

'I'm sure you do, and I've nothing personal against the boy. But both his father and I', Karen felt a familiar twinge of sadness as she thought about Gordon, 'would much prefer it if you and Sam had nothing to do with each other. We feel' – she searched uncomfortably for a suitable phrase, suddenly wondering if they were actually doing the right thing – 'it would be better for you both to have other friends.

'Jodie, things happened a long time ago between Sam's father and myself. I'll be perfectly honest with you.' She realised she had no chance of keeping the girl's love and respect if she wasn't. 'Gordon Miller loved me very much. He wanted to marry me. At one point I even thought I probably loved him, too. We *were* lovers,' Karen felt her face flush and mentally scolded herself for being such a prude, 'in every sense of the word. But I was very young, not much older than you.

'When your dad breezed into my life he simply took me over. I couldn't think straight because I'd never met anyone like him before. I'd only known him a week when he decided he was going to marry me!

'Gordon', Karen gulped, remembering the scene that had happened all those years ago as clearly as if it had just happened, 'told me I was being a fool. He warned me that Bob Mitchenson wasn't a one-woman man and that sooner or later he'd simply walk out on me and leave me flat, which is precisely what happened, of course.

'I told *him* he was just a stuck-up old idiot.' Despite herself she could feel tears threatening at the back of her throat. 'I said he'd never do anything with his life except doze it away in this silly little village, commuting back and forward to his precious teaching job in Manchester, and eventually retiring on his pension, growing roses and cooing over his grandchildren.

'It was a vicous set of things to say, and he very properly slapped my face for it and suggested I stop acting like a slut.

'We had a row.' She blinked the tears away and tried to focus on Jodie. 'The most bloody and awful row I've ever had with anyone, including your dad.

'In the end he said he never wanted to see me again, and that he was sad he'd been foolish enough to let himself fall in love with someone as petty-minded and ridiculous as me.

'I told him if I was ridiculous, he was pathetic, and walked out.

'Your nan', Karen searched in her pocket desperately for a tissue, blindly wondering if the depths of emotion she was feeling were reaching Jodie at all, 'blamed him for everything else that happened. She hasn't spoken to him for years and still won't.

'Jodie,' she reached her hand out to the girl, who walked towards her slowly and took it, 'all the things that happened, all the things that were said and done before you were born go far too deep and still hurt far too much for either Gordon or I to risk them happening again between you and Sam.

'I know, I know,' she heard rather than saw Jodie sink on to the edge of Pia's bed, 'you and he are different people. I know the times and the circumstances and everything else are different, too. But neither Sam's father nor I could feel comfortable knowing you and Sam were seeing each other and perhaps getting swept up in the same kind of young emotions we were once swept along by.

'Can you understand that?' She found the tissue and blew her nose hard.

'No.' Jodie's voice was very calm, very cold and sounded very mature in the stillness of the room. 'Sam and I like each other. We like being with each other. But we're *us*! We're not something that happened back in the sixties!

'I'm not you and I never could be. I've got to make my own mistakes, so stop trying to save me by telling me all about yours!

'You and Mr Miller couldn't work things out, fine!

That's your problem.' Karen felt her snatch her hand away. 'You and Dad made a mess of things, I'm sorry, but it's nothing to do with me!

'I'm not going to promise never to see Sam, Mum. I couldn't possibly keep that promise in a place this size anyway.

'I'm me, and I've got enough problems just being that. So leave me alone, please!' Then with a stifled sob she raced out and Karen heard the bathroom door slam and lock behind her. Seconds later there was the sound of the bath filling with water and Jodie's Walkman turned to full pounding rock volume.

'Is it a private argument, or can anyone throw things?' Pia sidled round the door, her ten-year-old face puckered into a frown. 'I heard Jodie shouting and I wasn't sure which one of you maybe needed help.

'Mum!' She suddenly noticed the tears trickling down Karen's cheeks and rushed to hug her. 'What's the matter? What's happened?'

'Nothing special.' Karen sniffed, feeling younger than her younger daughter and ten times more vulnerable. 'And what on earth are you doing wearing that jacket? It used to be your grandad's gardening jacket! Where did you find it?'

'In the cellar with a lot of dusty flowerpots,' Pia shrugged. 'All I did was try it on. Then I heard the racket up here and thought maybe I should come join in. I'll go and take it off if you like?'

'Oh, Pia!' In spite of herself, Karen laughed. The girl looked so ridiculous standing there in a dirty, patched tweed jacket that should have been thrown out years ago that even the angry music from the bathroom seemed to fade into the background. 'Sometimes I wonder about you! Are you ten, or really a hundred? And what are you honestly going to grow up into?'

'Queen of the entire world?' Pia suggested modestly. 'I could start off with that and then go in for space once they've got the shuttle sorted out. What d'you think?'

'I think it's time we went downstairs and you poured me that whisky you "accidentally" found before Nan gets back.' Karen pulled herself stiffly to her feet, feeling the aches of tension in her shoulders and neck and wishing, for the umpteenth time, Bob Mitchenson – or someone like him – was still around to help her cope.

'Maybe', she thought as she and Pia trudged downstairs in single file, 'it really *is* impossible to be a single-parent family, particularly if you're the parent to two growing-up girls. Maybe I need to put my name down with one of those computer marriage bureaux, the way Bob's folks suggested in Sydney, and find the ideal mate who'll be able to share all the stresses and strains and reassure me I'm doing the right thing.

'Or maybe,' she glanced over her shoulder at the firmly bolted bathroom door, 'Jodie's the one who's right and Gordon and I are wrong. Maybe we should just let Sam and her continue seeing each other and cross our fingers that it all works out OK.'

She sank down into the sofa, only vaguely registering Pia bustling in the background with glasses and a bottle, closed her eyes and wondered – through the beginnings of a thumping headache – how different things would have been if she'd never met Bob Mitchenson, and never seen Australia.

Chapter 6

Pia put the glass of whisky carefully on to the coffee-table, checked that her mother was as preoccupied as she looked, then padded quietly across the room and closed the door behind her.

'Hey!' she hissed softly at the bathroom door. 'Open up! It's only me!'

'Go away,' Jodie mumbled, splashing water aimlessly round the bath to make it sound as if she were actually washing herself and not just sitting on the edge of the loo trying to stop crying.

'Don't come it! I know you're not *in* the bath! If you were in the bath you'd sound more echoey and water-logged, and you don't, you just sound hiccuppy. Come on. Let me in.' She bent and wiggled her fingers through the gap at the bottom of the door. 'If you don't, I'll tell Nan how you used her Chanel Number Five the day Sam took you for a walk along the Edge!'

'Pia, for Pete's sake!' The bolt was shot back and Jodie eased the door open enough for her sister to slip through. 'You're not being funny. Not after all that business with Mum!'

'Never said I was.' Pia windmilled herself in a hap-hazard circle to try to get rid of the steam. 'But I'd guess you're going to need a mate shortly, and the only one you're likely to get round here is me. So maybe you'd better start treating me properly and telling me just what *is* going on.'

She balanced herself precariously on the edge of the bath, folded her arms and stared at her sister.

'There's Mum downstairs looking like she's just had a fight with a six-foot-long goanna and lost. There's you up here acting as if you've found a redback under the bed and it's getting ready to bite you, and there's me in the middle,' she indicated herself with an airy wave of her arm, almost knocking over some cosmetic jars, 'who just wants to live a nice peaceful life and not have to go to that awful school, *or*', she pouted, 'spend my time freezing to death because this stupid country can't get its seasons right!'

'Oh Pia!' Jodie suddenly giggled hysterically, turning to face her sister. 'You're impossible! And what on earth d'you think you're almost wearing?'

'It's the very latest in extremely ancient off-the-shoulder gardening jackets.' Pia pirouetted to show the effect. 'I found it in the cellar where I was having a mooch. According to Mum, it was Grandad's. I thought it might do for this model-man thing some of the kids in the village are making to burn on November 5th.'

'If it was Grandad's and it's still around, Nan's likely to kill you if you do anything like that with it. I'd put it back and forget it if I were you. You know what she's like.'

'Sure. I know.' Pia unbuttoned the jacket and shrugged it to the floor. 'It was only a thought anyway. Now come one. Just *tell* me what's happening. Please,' she wheedled. 'If you do, I'll smuggle you up a bit of Nan's egg and bacon pie, which doesn't taste as awful as it sounds, and I guess you're *starving* by now, aren't you? Or does all this love business really affect your appetite the way they say in those corny books?'

'*What* love business?' Jodie glared at her, mopping her face with a wet flannel.

'Well, aren't you in love with Sam Miller and isn't that what all the fuss is about?' Pia grinned, far too innocently.

'I just don't *know*!' Jodie almost wailed. 'I like Sam. Sure! I like him a lot. And I don't see why I've got to stop meeting him just because his dad and Mum made a mess of things centuries ago!'

She faced Pia, leaning against the sink. 'I – I'm all knotted-up inside. I don't know what to feel any more, and I'm beginning to think I *hate* this place, and Nan, and Mum, and everybody else in it! I'd like to run away and smuggle myself on board a ship or a plane that was heading for Sydney Harbour!'

'Well, *I* think', Pia stared at her unblinkingly, 'what you should do is talk to Sam about it all. He's probably had the same lecture tonight.

'Personally,' she straightened and wiped her own face with a towel, 'it seems to be storms in egg cups and moles into mountains. What you need', she waggled her finger sternly at Jodie, 'is to get out and about a bit more like me.

'The other kids round here aren't brilliant, but they're not quite as dumb as they look, either. Maybe you should take up Nan's offer and go on a secretarial course to Manchester or something. At least it'd stop you flopping round the house all day like that old cat.

'But right this minute, know what I reckon you should do?'

Jodie shook her head dumbly, feeling a mixture of exasperation and respect for the younger girl. Pia always had had an uncanny knack of putting things into perspective. Sometimes it wasn't exactly the kind of perspective adults like Mum or Dad or Nan would appreciate, but it was always better than nothing, and it always helped. Like when Jodie's favourite cat on the farm had died and a six-year-old Pia had staggeringly told her it wasn't dead at all, it had just gone bush and would probably reappear in one of the gum trees as a koala bear or a parrot. Three days later a koala had, indeed, mysteriously appeared fleetingly in one of the gum trees, and ever since then Jodie had viewed Pia with a certain amount of unacknowledged respect.

Her words cut through Jodie's memories. 'I reckon you ought to sneak back to the bedroom while I go be my entertaining self downstairs and keep everybody away from you. Then you can write a letter to Sam and arrange to meet him someplace.'

Jodie frowned. 'And how is that supposed to help any little thing? How do I get the stupid letter to him when I'm not supposed to see him?'

'We-ell, if the price was right, like if I could borrow your fluffy waistcoat for this Guy Fawkes party I'm going to, I guess I could just find myself wandering round by Sam's dad's place collecting dead twigs and sticks for the bonfire!'

'But if Mum found *that* out,' Jodie sagged against the sink again, 'and I mean, I couldn't possibly meet him anywhere round here or somebody'd be certain to gossip about it, it could all get *awful*, Pia!'

'It could all get awful anyway!' Pia shrugged carelessly. 'And anyway, you wouldn't *have* to meet him round here. You could tell them you were taking me into Manchester on something boringly cultural, like a trip round a museum maybe, then I could get lost and you and Sam could meet on the Edge.

'Of course,' she said consideringly, 'it *would* mean I'd have to have a certain amount of cash to get lost with! But I know you've been saving up to buy me a birthday pressie anyway, so this could just be a first instalment, couldn't it?'

Jodie glared at her, wondering whether or not to strangle her with the face flannel – along with all the other talents she kept producing, occasionally Pia showed all the signs of becoming the biggest small wheeler dealer this side of the equator. Then slowly she nodded, the sick feeling inside her turning to a churning excitement.

'Deal!' She spat into her palm, rubbed it against her side and held it out to Pia.

'Deal!' Pia repeated the action, then they solemnly shook hands.

Chapter 7

The next afternoon was wet and windy, and Jodie shivered in her good, but thin, coat as she and Pia stood at the bus stop.

The letter had been delivered. Jodie's almost sulky suggestion that she pass the time somehow by taking

Pia to look at Gawsworth Hall before it closed for the winter had been greeted with a raised eyebrow from Nan, and a relieved smile from their mother.

'If we can't get in or anything, at least we can have a look at the outside, and I want to see Maggoty Johnson's Wood. There's a jester buried there,' Pia had explained seriously, winking sideways at the astonished Jodie.

'Don't be too late,' Karen had called to them as they'd sauntered a lot more casually than they'd felt down the garden path. 'Nan doesn't mind if you miss tea for once, but you've got to be in for supper.'

'Ugh!' Pia had muttered into her anorak which, despite everybody's efforts, she'd refused to be parted from. 'Black pudding, fried egg and oven chips, all running in grease! Hasn't this place ever *heard* of steaks and proper hamburgers?'

'Shut up!' Jodie had nudged her. 'And what's all this Maggoty Johnson business?'

'Just a bit of homework I did for both of us as neither of us is going *near* Gawsworth thingummy, but I guessed it might be sensible if we had some facts and figures to spout when we came home! Good thinking, huh?' she'd grinned.

'Brilliant!' Jodie had murmured reluctantly. 'But just where *are* you going?'

Pia had glared sideways at her. 'I am planning a very cultural afternoon with Ken Roberts and his two brothers. I'm going to thrash them at pinball, because they've got a machine in their garage, and none of them knows how to play it properly!'

'Oh, Pia, I'm sure this isn't right, you know. I'm sure we're both going to get into terrible trouble, and probably Sam, *and* Ken Roberts – whoever he is – and everybody else as well! Maybe we should forget the whole thing. Maybe we really should catch the bus for Macclesfield.'

'And maybe pigs should fly!' Pia had stuck her tongue out at her. 'Listen, you need to sort something out with Sam, even if it's only how you're really feeling about him. *I* need to get away from that cottage.

'Did you know,' she'd added thoughtfully, 'I over-heard Nan telling Mum it was time I started taking piano lessons? Can you imagine it? Me? On a piano? With Nan teaching? Have you ever watched her when she's been playing? Her fingers look like a funnal web spider when it's going in for the kill, the way they sort of rear up at the keys! That just isn't my scene at all. Thanks, but no thanks! When did you last hear any of our mates in Sydney having *piano* lessons? And all that musty old sheet music! The most recent thing she's got's Beethoven, and he's been dead for yonks! Pretty much like this place really, when you think about it,' she'd sighed, cuddling her chin further down in her anorak.

'D'you ever suppose', she said wistfully as the local bus approached, 'we're going to actually *like* England, Jodie? I mean, don't you ever miss home and the fact that it's the start of summer back there, and we should be eating strawberries and surfing and staying out on the beach all night instead of shivering in our socks like this? Doesn't it ever get to you?'

'Sometimes,' Jodie admitted, helping Pia on to the bus and then standing back as the automatic doors clunked shut. They'd agreed where they'd meet up later and Pia had assured her that Ken Roberts and his brothers wouldn't say a word about her being in Nether Alderley with them instead of Macclesfield with Jodie.

'For Pommies, they're not bad really,' she'd shrugged. 'And they're even newer than us to the district so nobody's going to make the connection anyway. Relax and enjoy yourself,' she'd leered, tweaking her sister's coat-sleeve. 'And don't do anything Mum wouldn't!'

But Mum, Jodie was almost certain as she finally wandered down the track towards the place Sam had suggested, would never have done this. She'd never really have gone behind Nan's back, or disobeyed Nan's express orders – not until she met Bob Mitchenson, anyway!

The rain was easing slightly, slipping away over the patchwork fields like mist, and a thin, suddenly wintery sun struggled weakly through the clouds.

She sat down on a rock, pulling her coat more closely to her and wishing she'd worn a thicker sweater instead of her thin tracksuit top and skirt. But bundling into a dozen sweaters to trail round a stately home might have brought raised eyebrows – Nan had almost had a heart attack anyway when she'd first appeared downstairs in jeans and flat-heeled shoes.

No self-respecting granddaughter of *hers*, she'd announced firmly, was going to the home of the Dark Lady of the Sonnets looking like a gypsy, so Jodie could change immediately, please.

Now, sitting here in the late October light, she felt like a misfit – not just to the clothes she was wearing, but to the entire gentle sweep of the countryside with its drifting, yellowing leaves and toy-town fields.

Once, back on the farm when her dad had caught her sitting in a corner by the outbuildings, scribbling her thoughts into a battered old exercise book, he'd grabbed it away from her and shouted that writing words and drawing endless pictures, the way she had done, was just a waste of time.

'What good'll it do you when you're grown-up?' he'd yelled, tearing the book in half and ignoring her tears and protests. 'Who fills your head with all this nonsense? You don't get it from my side of the family, that's for sure!

He'd shaken her by the shoulders until she'd winced with pain. 'Maybe you fancy yourself as some refined English lady taking tea on the lawn and nibbling cucumber sandwiches?

'Well, Australia isn't like that, kid! It's not a country for your kind of dreamer, and the sooner you find that out, the better you'll be. *You're* an Australian, not a wishy-washy Pom who can't tell the time of day without a wrist-watch!'

Suddenly she felt her eyes fill with tears.

She didn't feel Australian. And she didn't feel English. She simply felt lost and lonely and, more important, *alone* – as if someone had stuck her inside a goldfish bowl where all she could do was stare through the glass endlessly knowing she'd never actually be able to touch the world outside.

'Hi!' The hand on her shoulder made her jump, and she spun round guiltily, almost falling. 'Come on. Let's get a bit further into the woods. We're too public here as we're not supposed to be seen together.'

Sam was smiling down at her worriedly, as if he were no more sure than she that they should both be there.

She scrambled to her feet, brushing her hair out of her eyes. But at least he was here! At least he was *real*!

'I – I had to talk to you,' she mumbled. 'It's all been getting silly at the cottage.'

'I know. I guess we've both had the same treatment.' He reached out his hand tentatively and took hold of hers. 'Jodie, it's stupid. The whole thing's stupid. I feel like we're both trapped in the middle of some crazy film or something.

'I want to see you. I want to be with you. And everybody else', he shrugged, desperation showing in every line of his body, 'thinks that's some kind of unnatural act. Is it?' He pulled her round to face him. 'Do you think it is?'

The thin ray of sunlight suddenly broadened as the wind picked up and chased the clouds further apart, scattering them across the sky like pieces of rag.

'No,' she whispered, her free hand reaching out to take his. 'I like you. I like you a lot, and I like being with you. I' – she hesitated, staring down at the ground – 'don't know if it's more than that, but I've never felt like this about anybody else before, so it's got to mean *something*.'

She smiled at him shyly, 'I don't even know if it's a something that lasts, but it's here at the moment, and it's real enough.'

They started to walk slowly, heading for a bank of trees. 'Back home, we don't have all these conventions you seem to have. We hang around together, we go out together, it's more relaxed. Just accepted. Here, it's like I ought to send you a formal invite to Sunday tea. Only', she added sadly, 'I'd never be allowed to have you over the doorstep.

'I don't understand any of it! I don't *want* any of it!' Her voice rose angrily, startling a ring dove into jagged flight. 'I just want for us both to be allowed to get on with our lives in our own ways. No interference. No scenes. No meeting like this, all secret and guilty. Because that's how I feel. Don't you?'

Her eyes, Sam noticed, were larger than ever and far too bright, as if the tears hiding in the corners were acting as reflectors and not only magnifying, but mirroring, the confused pain charging through them both.

'Yes,' he murmured. 'That's exactly how I feel.'

He dropped her right hand, put his arm round her waist and pulled her to him, panicking in case she backed away.

Then suddenly she was there, the squirrel eyes frowning, her long fingers touching his hair, almost frightened, her mouth turning down at the corners as the bewilderment at the whole situation showed in her entire face.

'I think, Jodie,' he whispered, feeling her breath on his cheek, 'I love you. I don't think I know what I mean when I say it, except that I've never felt like this before about anyone or anything, either, and if the way I'm feeling isn't love, then I don't know what else it can be.

'I also think', he tightened his grip round her shyly, 'I'm going to kiss you. That's if you don't mind and would like me to?'

'Please!' She nodded and a tear trickled down the inside of her nose.

He brushed it away gently.

Nothing moved. No birds sang. No wind rustled the grass. The earth didn't stop spinning. But as they moved further into each other's arms and their lips met for the first time, each of them felt their own tensions relax.

Whatever happened next, at least this one moment was real.

Chapter 8

'It's odd.' Sam put his arms gently round her shoulders as they continued to walk down the steep incline that smelled of tangled damp bracken and earth. 'The first time I saw you in the shop I thought there was something special about you.

'After Mum died I was so lonely. It was like she'd left me because she just didn't care any more. And the more I was with other people, the lonelier I got.'

He grinned at her and felt her move closer to him. 'Now I don't feel that way at all. Even when I can't see you, you still seem to be around inside my head. It's almost as if . . . ' He hesitated, the grin giving way to sudden seriousness, '. . . as if I've found a bit of myself that I've been missing for years, like an arm or a leg or something. Does that make sense?'

They stopped and looked at each other, while a real grey squirrel surveyed them nervously from the edge of the clearing. Then Jodie nodded and the squirrel, deciding they weren't any threat after all, scurried round in circles hiding nuts away for the winter with its front paws.

'I've always been lonely.' The girl's voice was soft and grating at the same time. 'Pia's great as a sister, but in spite of the way she behaves sometimes, she is still only little. I can't really talk to her, not about important things. She thinks she understands and, well, maybe sometimes she does. But I can't really expect somebody who's six years younger than me to give proper help and advice, can I?'

Sam didn't answer. Instead, he took off his bomber jacket, spread it carefully out on the least wet-looking patch of ground, and sat down, shyly pulling Jodie with him.

'When we first got here,' Jodie tucked her knees up to her chin and rested her arms on them, 'Pia was the one who went out and met people and raced around. She always seemed to be doing something, while I was just slouching about with Nan's cat.

'It was the same when we moved to Sydney from the farm. Pia had all the neighbours sussed inside a week! She knew which ones owned their own dinghies down in the harbour, and who had a surfboard, and where the next barbecue was going to be.'

'And what did you do?' Sam moved away from her slightly, desperately wanting to reach out and kiss her again, and not trusting himself to even touch her.

'I sat in Gramp's garden and watched the parrots or counted the frogs jumping into the pool. Once,' she added, her eyes clouded and far away, 'I saw a toad try to eat a stag beetle. The beetle hissed at it and the toad hopped off.

'I didn't like that beetle. It was too big and black and ugly-looking. But I felt sorry for the toad. It had just wanted its supper, like everybody else. I burst into tears, and when Mum asked me what the matter was, I couldn't even explain, so she sent me to bed and told me to stop being so dramatic.

'But it wasn't being dramatic. That toad had such a sad look on his face I wanted to help him. But I never saw him again. Or if I did, I didn't recognise him.

'Pia told me I was crazy. That once the porch lights were on and all the insects were flying about, he'd have *more* than enough to eat. Somehow it didn't make any difference. I knew how that toad felt when its supper started fighting back with it. D'you understand?' She glanced at him, face flushing with embarrassment. 'Does it make sense? Any of it?'

'Yes.' Sam nodded slowly, then reached out and took her hand. 'It's being the one who's on the outside all the time, just staring in. You never seem to get to be part of the other people. And you know, all the time, it's really *you* who's stopping you, not anyone else. That's what you mean, isn't it?'

'Yes.' It was Jodie's turn to nod seriously. 'But I've never been able to explain it before.

'Sam,' she hesitated and her long fingers curled round his hand tightly, 'you know what we were talking about earlier, about other feelings and about you thinking you could maybe be in love with me? Well,' she took a deep breath and stared downhill away from him, 'I think maybe the way I'm feeling means I love you, too. But where does that leave us? What can we do if your dad and my mum and nan won't even let us see each other?'

'I don't know.' He felt hopeless and helpless and far too young. 'I'll talk to Dad again. He's never acted this way before. Maybe you could talk to your mum?'

'No!' She shook her head vehemently and her hair fell forward like a heavy blanket. 'She won't listen and I – I think she'd rather send me away to secretarial school or something than risk anything starting up between you and me.

'But something *has* started, hasn't it?' She faced him, her eyes the colour of the wet bracken rustling in the wind behind them, and her entire face puckered into a confused frown.

He let her hand go and put his arms round her, drawing her to him, needing the reassurance of her warmth and touch and the bony angles of her own body under its clothes close to his.

He didn't want to make love to her; didn't want to fool around with her in the half-hearted way he had with other girls. He simply wanted to hold her close and somehow protect her from everything that was hurting them both.

'Sam?' Her fingers touched his cheek and he opened his eyes, wishing he had at least some of the answers.

'Something's started all right,' he murmured, kissing her nose. 'And I'm not going to let you go, Jodie! Whatever happens, I'm not doing that.

'I . . .' he fumbled clumsily for the words, 'I want to take care of you. I want to do what's right by you. I want to make you laugh,' he added simply, 'so that next time you see a toad you'll notice how wonderful and golden his eyes are, and not think he looks sad because he's missed his supper.

'Does *that* make sense?'

They were lying back on the jacket and a couple of small dead leaves had tangled in Jodie's hair. He picked them out carefully in case he hurt her.

'Thank you.' She smiled seriously. 'And I don't want you to be lonely ever again.' She reached across and traced the line of his jaw with her finger. 'I don't want you to ever think people have left you because they don't care any more.

'Will you take me to Mow Cop, Sam? Will you show me where you hid out when you were ten?'

'Maybe.' He caught her hand and kissed it. 'But until we can get everything else sorted out, how're we going to manage to meet at all?'

'Pia,' Jodie said simply. 'We'll use Pia. She'll be a sort of — a sort of go-between and alibi. She'll do it. She'll think it's a great giggle. And', her hand started stroking his face again, 'we can trust her. She won't say anything. She's not that kind of kiddy.'

She sat up, suddenly full of determination and enthusiasm. 'You work on your dad, and I'll try to work on Mum and Nan. We'll be all right! We'll win out. Families can't behave like this! Not in the 1980s!'

But, Sam gloomily thought later as he walked her back along the track to their original meeting place, what if their individual families *did* continue to carry on the way they had done?

Neither he nor Jodie, he was sure, was the kind of person who could enjoy living in the shadows and going behind other people's backs. They weren't runaways or rebels. They weren't trying to prove anything to the world. They were simply two lost, lonely individuals who'd had the good luck to bump into each other in a sleepy village store!

Pia was waiting glumly in the bus shelter, her ten-year-old face screwed up with cold, and her shoes and anorak covered in mud.

'What on earth', Jodie exploded, 'have *you* been doing? Mum's never going to believe you got looking like that simply walking round a stately home!'

'Well, Mum can go jump a puddle!' Pia glowered. 'And she can believe what she likes! I don't care! I hate this place! I'm freezing to death!'

'Sam, please,' Jodie turned to the boy desperately, 'have you got a rag or something we can clean her up with? If I take her home looking like that, it'll be the end of everything.'

Sam fumbled in his pocket for a handkerchief and silently handed it to Jodie, who spat on it and then sponged and brushed at the mud frantically.

'Jodie,' Pia hopped away from her, 'will you please *stop* it? Anyway, you don't look so clever yourself! Stately homes don't very often have leaves you sit down on, and they *certainly* don't', she bent and picked some wet grass and fronds of bracken from Jodie's heels, 'have many of *these* around!'

For a second, despite the near-seriousness of the situation, Sam felt himself stifle a laugh – she was so small and square and determined. 'Now I, on the other hand, have done something positive and helpful.'

She fumbled in her pocket and pulled out a crumpled glossy brochure for Gawsworth. 'I have managed to get a hold of *this* ! Ken's folks dragged them all round the place last week, so I can tell you about the paintings and the Tudor fireplace, and how the sash windows in the library were put in by the second Earl of Macclesfield in 1701! Don't you think I'll sound authentic?'

'Maybe!' Jodie glared at her. 'But what about the mud? Where's that supposed to have come from?'

'The tilting ground, of course!' Pia tossed her head

scornfully. 'It's been wet all day, hasn't it? Which means there's bound to be mud, doesn't it?

'Doesn't it, Sam?' she appealed to him, holding her head to one side and reminding him of a mynah bird he'd once seen in a pet shop in Stockport.

'I suppose so,' he shrugged, his stomach tightening at the thought of all the lies beginning. 'But just as a matter of interest, Pia, why *are* you covered in mud?'

'Ken Roberts told me I was an Aussie immigrant and ought to be back playing with the Abos. I told him he was a Pommie so-and-so.' She grinned. 'I swore. He'd made me so mad. So he hit me and I hit him back.' She shrugged, not in the least embarrassed. 'Then his brothers joined in and it was three against one. I won, I think,' she added hopefully. 'Anyway, I cut his lip, but I'm seeing them again tomorrow, so if you two want to slope off someplace, you'd better make your minds up now.'

Sam could feel Jodie looking at him pleadingly, and he stared down at the dirty concrete floor of the shelter, vividly aware of the old newspapers and empty crisp packets that had been blown in by the wind.

'Do you, Sam?' Jodie whispered, just touching his jacket with her elbow.

'Do *you*?' His throat felt tight, as if he were coming down with a cold, and he had to struggle to breathe evenly.

More than anything in the world he wanted to be with her, wanted to take up any excuse that would *allow* him to be with her. But this way . . .? Using deceit and lying by simply avoiding telling the whole truth . . .?

'Yes.' Her hand reached blindly for his, found it,

covered it and gripped it so hard he could feel her nails digging into his palm. 'We don't know how long we can go on without being found out, but however long we've got is what we should take. Isn't it?'

She looked at him squarely and he saw the challenge in the squirrel eyes; saw that he'd been right and that the brown shades disappeared altogether and the grey hardened into sparkling granite when she was as determined as she seemed to be now.

'Yes.' He could hear the bus trundling down the lane towards them, and panic suddenly shot through him. If someone on that bus recognised him, saw him with Jodie and Pia, word would be round the village in a matter of hours, and however much he might love the girl standing beside him, he also still loved his father and didn't want to hurt him any more than was necessary.

'Tomorrow then. Early. Is that possible, Pia?' He looked quickly at the ten-year-old, who winked at him and crammed a strip of chewing gum into her mouth.

'Where do we say we're visiting this time?' Jodie asked quietly, as if she'd guessed what had been going through his head. 'I mean, we can hardly be out all day seeing *another* ancient monument!'

'Say,' he stared at Pia, who stared back, chewing solemnly, 'say you met some friends of Pia's, the Roberts, and they've asked you for lunch! Would that do? Would *that* be possible?'

'Uh-uh!' Pia shook her head. 'Too easy for Mum to check. But if I said *I'd* been asked for lunch – which, as a matter of fact, I have! – then Jodie could offer to drop me there, but want to go shopping in Stockport and take in a movie or something before she picked me up again. How would that grab anybody?'

'Fine!' Sam reached across and kissed Jodie quickly.
'If you can pull it off, great! I'll meet you here. About
ten. The bus doesn't come till twenty-past, so we'll be
clear. If Dad isn't using the car, I'll see if I can borrow
it, say I want to go and take a look round for some
more casual work now winter's coming in.

'I'll pick you both up. We can drive Pia to Nether
Alderley.' He was talking quickly, the words hurrying
over each other and his Cheshire accent becoming
more pronounced so Jodie had to strain to understand
him.

'I'd better go.' He didn't want to leave her, but the
noise of the bus was closer. 'I'll see you tomorrow.' His
own face softened as he watched her frown. 'OK?
You'll *be* OK, won't you?' he added anxiously.

'We'll be fine.' It was Pia who answered. Jodie had
simply moved closer to him, put her arms round his
neck and was tilting her face up to his.

'We'll be more than fine!' she whispered, and he
knew she wasn't referring to the bus trip or whatever
the evening ahead brought all of them.

'I love you,' he mumbled inadequately into her hair,
holding her to him as if she were a piece of precious
crystal that might snap in two at any second.

'Love you, too.' Her lips touched his and the tip of
her tongue gently, hesitantly, pushed against his partly
opened mouth.

Then the bus's headlights swept across the top of the
hill towards them, and he felt Jodie push him away
quickly.

'Go on!' she said breathlessly. 'I'll see you in the
morning!'

Seconds later Pia, clutching the Gawsworth Hall brochure, demurely mounted the steps to the local bus. Jodie followed, peering back through the sudden darkness and the rain that had started again.

But Sam had disappeared as completely as if he'd never existed, and she sank back into her seat with a sigh of relief.

Pia hissed anxiously, 'Are you sure you two know what you're doing?'

'No.' She shook her head, trying to stop the smile that was threatening to take her over and develop into a hysterical giggle. 'No, Pia, I'm not sure of anything. And neither is Sam. But,' she looked at her sister, 'we've got to have time to find out. OK?'

'OK, possum!' Pia attempted to blow a bubble with the chewing gum, failed and pulled it out of her mouth in disgust. 'Just don't blame me if it all goes wrong, will you?'

Chapter 9

In some ways, the next four weeks were the happiest Jodie had ever known.

She didn't see Sam often, but the meetings they did manage to arrange had a particular excited sweetness about them, and they both held on to their moments together, hugging them to them and storing them away in their minds so they could bring them out privately when they were alone and relive them.

Jodie had even found herself doing crazy things like going to Bolton for a day because Sam was working there, and then getting soaking wet just wandering round the centre of the town waiting for him to finish so they could at least have some time together on the return journey home.

Even the strange November 5th party on the village green had been special.

She'd been there, standing between her mum and nan, clutching Pia's hand and staring through the sea of sparks and flickering yellow-blue flames from the bonfire towards where Sam would've been if Gordon Miller hadn't dragged him off to Sheffield on some kind of business.

Pia had suddenly nudged her violently, just as some rockets had exploded into trails of stars.

'He's here!' she'd hissed, handing her a sparkler. 'And so's his dad. Don't look round, but he can't take his eyes off you, Jodie! And', the younger girl had jumped up and down, leaving her own stream of gunpowder stars behind her, 'Mum can't seem to take her eyes off Mr Miller! She's all flushed, and I don't think it's anything to do with the fireworks!'

Later there had been a polite confrontation over the charred baked potatoes and half-cooked sausages.

'Enjoying it, Karen?' Gordon Miller had been very proper, smiling vaguely at no one in particular.

'Brings back memories, I suppose.' Karen Mitchenson had smiled, a bit wistfully Jodie had thought, then concentrated her efforts on trying to find the flesh inside the potato's skin with a plastic fork.

'Yes.' Gordon had turned away abruptly. 'Nothing

really changes, does it?'

Before Karen could answer, Pia had choked, and Jodie had led her quickly away from the crowds, thumping her on the back and asking anxiously if she was all right.

''Course I am!' her sister had hissed. 'Just acting, dumbo!'

'Why?' Jodie had been genuinely puzzled, until she'd felt Sam's firm hands on her waist and heard him whisper, 'I missed you. I love you.'

The warmth from his words had careered through her. He was all, it seemed, she really needed – someone who cared. Someone who was there.

She'd never been able to talk to her mother, even in the old days – The B.E. Days, Before England, as she privately called them.

Pia would bounce round the farm, or the house in Sydney, telling everyone what was on her mind and how her day had been. Jodie had never been able to put her feelings into words she'd thought anyone would understand. And her mum in turn, she'd realised, had left the girl to herself, judging it might be better, taking the adult's way out because she hadn't known any more than Jodie what *she* should be saying.

'Love you, too.'

She hadn't dared look at Sam. She'd concentrated on Pia, now overacting hopelessly. Then she'd felt his lips on the back of her neck under her hair just as the night sky had exploded into a zipping rainbow of light with the grand set piece finale.

There had been a collective gasp of appreciation from the villagers, then the darkness had trailed back – and Sam had gone again.

'OK?' Pia had looked at her and grinned. 'I can't choke much longer, I'm afraid. It's starting to hurt my throat!'

She'd suddenly found herself hugging her sister, tears threatening to trickle over as the almost tangible loneliness crept back round her.

'You sure you're OK?' Pia's small grubby hand had tugged at her arm. 'You'd better find a smile to pin on your face from someplace, because you can't go back to Mum and Nan looking like *that*. You're supposed to've been *enjoying* yourself, remember?'

But when they'd drifted casually into the thinning crowds round the bonfire, Mum and Nan had already left because, a neighbour had informed them, Mrs Wright was beginning to feel cold.

Jodie shivered suddenly at the memories, staring out at the lowering yellow clouds over the bare trees.

Nan had just said it was going to snow.

'You can smell it,' she'd murmured, watching Jodie carefully weigh raisins, dates and sultanas for the Christmas mincemeat they were making.

'You've never seen snow, have you?'

Jodie had shaken her head while Edward had yowled toothlessly round both their ankles, convinced that the mixture being assembled was his supper.

'I don't suppose Australia gets much, although I read somewhere that there's an area called the Snowy Mountains where you can ski occasionally. Still, it must be extremely peculiar eating Christmas lunch with temperatures in the hundreds!'

Jodie had never really thought about it. All her life Christmas had been in the middle of summer. It had never seemed in the least bit strange to start Christmas morning with a swim and then sit down to turkey and Christmas pudding and brandy butter in the evening when it was cooler.

'We get cut off here sometimes.' The old woman's voice had been conversational, almost friendly.

'Jodie,' she'd hesitated, carefully peeling the apples for the mincemeat while Edward had brushed his tail against her leg in unnecessary anticipation, 'I know you must feel – well, strange, particularly now Pia's at school and you're on your own all day. We'll really have to decide on some kind of job for you in the New Year. But you are basically all right, aren't you?'

Barbara Wright shifted her position painfully.

It was cold, bitterly cold, and the clouds scudding across the sky outside the window were a sure sign of bad weather. She suddenly felt very sorry for her granddaughter.

It wasn't Jodie's fault she'd been brought up the way she had, and apart from all that nonsense when Karen had thought she and Sam Miller were seeing each other – and when Jodie herself had been behaving like a moody little nothing – the girl was pleasant to have around, particularly recently.

She made the effort to be cheerful and helpful, which was much more, if the truth were told, than Karen had ever done at the same age.

Barbara grunted impatiently and Jodie jumped guiltily, frowning at her.

'I asked if you were all right. Kindly answer.' Her hip hurt and she felt irritable. This time of year was always the same. There was always far too much to organise before Christmas.

'I – I'm sorry, Nan.' Jodie bent and fussed Edward between his ears until his face stretched into a purring cat-smile. 'I'm fine. There isn't anything wrong with me. Honestly.'

'I didn't imply there was. I merely asked a question.' Grandmother glared at granddaughter angrily, and Jodie felt herself stiffen.

Then suddenly Barbara Wright relaxed and smiled. 'It would be so nice', she said, chopping up the peeled apples and putting them in a saucepan, 'if your first Christmas here were a white Christmas.

'When your grandfather, God rest his soul, and I were married and your mother was just a little baby, our first Christmas as a family was a white Christmas. I'll never forget it.

'I was coming back from the village on Christmas Eve. Everywhere was white, and it was just starting up again. We had a tree in the window covered in tinsel and fairy-lights. I came in through the gate and there was your grandfather at the window, holding Karen so she could see the snowflakes. Her little hands kept touching the glass, trying to catch them, and Bill was laughing at her.'

Barbara's face softened, and Jodie found herself watching the old woman in fascination.

It had never really occurred to her that her grand-parents, or her mum and dad, might once have cared for each other the same way she and Sam cared.

'Nan,' she hesitated, 'Mum never talks about Grandad. What was he like? I don't think I've ever even seen a photograph of him.'

Barbara Wright laughed, then sat down heavily in the kitchen chair.

'He was a charmer,' she said simply. 'We went to school together, then he lied about his age and ran away and joined the navy. I forgot all about him until one morning I walked into the local shop. It was just after the war and we still had ration books. There was a very tall young man standing there holding a tin of powdered milk as if he'd never seen anything so disgusting in his life.

'He smiled at me – he had very blue eyes – and said, "You've grown up well, Barbara!"

'We were married that autumn, in the village church.

'The most precious thing in his life, after he left the navy, was your mother. Fortunately,' Barbara's voice turned suddenly cold, 'he died before he could see what a mess she finally got herself into.'

'Was my dad really that bad?' Jodie leaned against the table, only half of her concentrating on the answer when it came. The other half was thinking about Sam, wondering where he was and what he was doing.

'Bad isn't exactly the right word.' Her grandmother sounded thoughtful. 'He was different, like Bill, and he was the wrong kind of person for your mother. She always needed a firm hand, and when your grandfather was alive, although he adored her, he was strict with her.'

Barbara stood up painfully. 'Maybe it was all my fault. Perhaps I didn't cope as well as I thought I did. But it was Gordon Miller's fault, too! He knew the whole truth,' she added bitterly. Then, leaning heavily on her stick, she crossed to the kitchen door and went out, slamming it behind her.

Jodie sighed, feeling her body sag against the table, its rough wooden side cutting into her and the sweet smell from the mixed fruit and the brandy making her stomach churn over.

Just for a second she'd hoped she was going to find out what had really happened. Just for a second Barbara Wright had seemed ready to talk to her openly, and if that had happened Jodie knew she would've told her grandmother about Sam and herself: would've confessed she was still seeing him, and would go on seeing him whatever anybody said, because she loved him.

But the second had disappeared. The opportunity had faded the way the daylight was fading, and the little surge of expectancy that had charged through her had been blotted out.

'Oh, Edward!' She bent down and scooped up the old cat, who wriggled protestingly at the indignity, then settled into her arms with his head under her chin. '*Why* does it have to be like this? Why can't I just put on my coat now, turn round and tell Nan I'm going to meet Sam? Why've we both got to lie all the time? It isn't fair! It just isn't fair!'

'What isn't fair?'

Karen Mitchenson was tired. Her feet hurt and she had the beginnings of a headache. The Manchester stores had been packed with Christmas shoppers, and if she heard one more taped recording of 'Silent Night' she thought she would probably go mad. 'Why are you here, anyway? I thought you were meeting Pia from school the way you normally do.'

'Oh, hi Mum!' Jodie put Edward carefully down on his place on the rug. 'I didn't hear you come in. Have a good shop?'

'No I didn't!' Karen snapped, pulling off her coat

72

and walking towards the electric kettle. 'I couldn't get any of the things your nan wanted, although why', she muttered under her breath, 'she wanted gold tinsel I *cannot* imagine! There's a box of the stuff in the cellar!'

She filled the kettle, plugged it in and sat down thankfully, unzipping the boots she'd bought and, mistakenly, decided to wear.

'What about Pia?' She massaged her calf, feeling the circulation starting to tingle through.

'She's got a rehearsal for a carol concert. I'm going to get her in a minute. But', Jodie carefully crossed her fingers against the lie and took a deep breath, 'she wasn't sure how long it might go on for. We could be a bit late.'

'Oh.' Karen glanced at her daughter suspiciously. 'And what are *you* supposed to do while she's cater-wauling?'

'Hang around and wait,' Jodie shrugged, concentrating on the gathering darkness beyond the window. 'Apparently that'll be OK. I can sit at the back of the hall and listen. I don't have to be outside or anything.'

The kettle boiled noisily, then switched itself off. 'Well, for Heaven's sake don't get a chill. It's freezing out there. I think it might snow, so wrap up warmly, and take an extra scarf with you. Neither of you is used to this kind of weather, and the last thing Nan and I need is you both in bed with colds.'

'Yes.' Jodie edged towards the door, hoping the guilt she was feeling didn't show in her face. 'Nan said she thought it would snow, too. I'll bet Pia's looking forward to that. She'll probably want to go sledging with the Roberts boys or something. It might even be fun,' she added wistfully.

'Jodie?' Karen poured boiling water over a teabag and swirled it round in her cup with a spoon. 'Are you OK? You seem a bit – well, on edge. Are you having your period or something?'

'Yes,' the girl answered truthfully, relieved that her mother thought her restlessness was something physical. 'I started this morning. Still,' she shrugged herself into the thick duffel coat her grandmother had brought back from a shopping expedition to Stockport, 'it means I'll be OK for Christmas, doesn't it? I'd better fly, Mum. I've just noticed the time. Pia could be waiting. 'Bye!'

She brushed her lips quickly against her mother's cheek, pulled open the back door and stepped out into the darkness, just as the first flakes of snow started to swirl down on the wind.

Chapter 10

She hurried along the path, feeling the snow licking at her face and settling on her eyelashes.

It was an extraordinary sensation, and she almost wanted to laugh aloud.

Because it was there, because you could see it and touch it, you expected it to make some kind of noise. But it simply filtered round you in complete silence, like dozens of delicate, inquisitive fingers, touching you briefly and then dancing away.

The village, when she reached it, looked like a drawing from a Charles Dickens book.

She half-expected to see a stage-coach and horses gallop towards her round the green where the Christmas tree that had already been put up shimmered with its lights, its branches already whitening.

The wind moaned in the hedges and the snow flurried in miniature whirlpools, some of the flakes that were almost touching the ground suddenly scurrying upwards as if they were drawn back in on themselves.

She stopped by the school lane, checked that the lights were still on in the hall and grinned to herself as a disjointed medley of children's voices announced that Good King Wenceslas had looked out.

She could imagine the ripple of excitement that had gone round the class when someone had first noticed it was snowing, and could almost see Pia's face. Her eyes would be imitating saucers and she would by now, Jodie guessed, have got very impatient at the fact that she was still caged up with all the others.

'But please,' she whispered, '*please* let the rehearsal take another half-hour, or at the very least, if it's *got* to finish, let them all have a game or something!'

She fumbled in her coat pocket for the note Pia had brought her the previous evening.

'*Meet me tomorrow, usual place. Urgent. I love you. Sam.*'

Pia had shaken her head when she'd asked about it.

'I didn't see him,' she'd said. 'I just checked the stone, the way you told me to, in case there were any messages. That was there.'

The stone was a large rock on the edge of the woods. Time, weather, and probably small animals had eaten away the ground on the far side of it, turning it into a natural hiding place.

The moment she and Sam had discovered it they'd made up their minds to use it as a post-box. It was close enough to the school for Pia to keep an eye on it, but hidden away enough for no one – unless they knew it was there – to suspect what it might actually be used for.

Jodie shivered.

She hadn't seen Sam for four days. The last time had been for a brief half-hour on Saturday afternoon when her mum and nan had gone to visit old Mrs Raffald.

Pia had been spending the day with the Roberts boys, who'd been given a puppy as an early Christmas present, and Jodie, alone in the cottage for the first time since they'd arrived in Cheshire, had taken her courage in both hands and dialled Sam's telephone number.

She'd let it ring four times. Put the phone down. Then redialled, praying Mr Miller wouldn't answer and that Sam was somewhere in earshot.

Like the messages at the stone, it was a code they'd worked out between them.

Four plus four meant Jodie was on her own and the coast was clear of both adults and Pia.

Three plus three meant Sam's dad had gone away for the day and that Sam would be in the workshop at the bottom of the garden if Jodie could get there without being seen.

Two plus three, from either of them, meant an emergency, and a meeting on the Edge as soon as they could make it, or a note left under the stone.

But he didn't ring, Jodie thought, hurrying forward through the snow. He just left the note! What's wrong?

What's happened?

Five minutes after she'd made the phone call on Saturday, there had been a tap on the kitchen door and when she'd rushed to answer it Sam had been standing there with a foolish smile on his face and a faded, fragile dog rose in his hand.

'I think it's the last one of the summer,' he'd murmured, kissing her gently. 'I found it tangled up with the brambles in the lane. I thought you ought to have it.'

'Oh, Sam!' She'd taken it from him carefully, superstitiously frightened in case the petals suddenly crumbled and fell between her fingers.

'You know what dog roses mean?' His arms had been round her and she'd snuggled into his warmth.

'No.' Her hair had curtained her face as she'd shaken her head.

'Pleasure and pain. At least, according to an old book of Mum's I was reading. That's right for us, isn't it?' His eyes had been cloudy and she'd suddenly noticed that the frown lines between his eyebrows seemed to have deepened over the last few weeks. He was too young to have frown lines that showed. They both were.

'But a lot of pleasure.' She'd put the rose down on the dresser, then hugged him to her, burying her face in his shoulder and feeling the tension in his spine under her fingers.

'So much pleasure!' she'd whispered, lifting her head eventually so he could kiss her.

They'd taken the rose and carried it upstairs.

Sam had watched while she'd folded a scrap of tissue paper round it and then pressed it carefully in a copy of

The Wind in the Willows that had been her mother's.

'I can't stay long,' he'd murmured, sitting on the edge of her bed and looking round the room, pulling in through his eyes the sights and the smells of it so he could picture her when he was alone in his own room. 'Dad thinks I've just popped down to the village to buy the local paper. He's busy in the workshop, finishing some stuff he's promised one of his customers for Christmas.

'Jodie,' he'd held out his hand, caught her by the arm and pulled her down beside him, 'what d'you want for Christmas? What can I get you that you can keep without anybody asking awkward questions about where it came from?'

'You've given me it already,' she'd answered simply, nodding towards the book. 'Pain and pleasure. And I'll have it for always.'

'The rose? Or the pain and the pleasure?' he'd asked, suddenly bitter.

'The rose — and the pleasure.' She'd lain back in his arms, closing her eyes and wishing with all her heart they could somehow find themselves alone on a desert island where they'd have all the time in the world to kiss and talk, and talk and kiss.

A gust of wind snatched at her scarf and the snow, as if it were playing games, drove fiercely into her face, forcing her to close her eyes.

She slipped on the uneven track, put her hands in front of her to steady herself, and felt her gloves drag against the surface of the stone.

'Sam?' she whispered, but the wind tore the word away.

'Jodie?' Suddenly he was beside her, a shape materialising out of nowhere.

'What is it? What's the matter?' Her teeth were chattering, but whether because she was cold or because she was scared she didn't know. 'I got your note. Pia brought it. I couldn't get out before now, and I can't stay. I've got to collect her from school.'

'I know. It's OK. I can't stay either.' He didn't make a move to touch her and in the eerie snow-light Jodie realised his face was tight with seriousness.

'Tell me,' she said quietly, letting her own arms hang by her sides.

He wiped snow from his face. 'On Saturday, someone saw me leaving the cottage. Don't ask me who. Dad wouldn't say.'

He glanced down at the rapidly whitening ground by his feet. 'There wouldn't be anything malicious about it. Just gossip. Someone asking what I was doing round at Barbara Wright's place, I suppose.'

'What did you say?' The cold seemed to have affected every part of her, including her lungs, because it had suddenly become increasingly difficult to breathe.

'I lied.' He shrugged. 'I told him whoever it was he'd been talking to must have been mistaken, that I'd gone to the village to buy the paper but they hadn't had one. And that on my way home I'd bumped into Vicky Dryden. She's a girl I went around with for a bit,' he explained apologetically. 'He seemed to believe me. At least he didn't ask me any more questions. But Jodie,' his voice cracked and he suddenly reached for her hand, 'I've never done that before. I've never told Dad a barefaced lie. I feel sick with myself.'

Jodie stood there rigidly, looking, Sam thought through his own confusion, exactly the way the Snow Queen should have looked — tall, beautiful, and somehow very remote. Then he felt her gloved fingers close firmly round his and sensed, rather than saw, the squirrel eyes harden into determination.

'I'm sorry.' The words hung in the snowflakes. 'It's not going to work, is it? Any of this? We can't go on the way we are doing, can we? If we do, we'll end up hating each other.

'Is that', she almost seemed to scream, 'what they want? Is that how they plan to keep us apart? Why?' She swung to face him and he saw the glint of tears on her cheeks. 'Why?' The near-scream died to a hopeless whisper.

'I don't know.' He felt inadequate. 'But I'm not blaming you. Don't think that. Please don't think that!' He pulled her to him. 'I just wanted to warn you. In case Dad didn't believe me after all. In case he gets on to your Mum. In case they find out about Pia and what she's been doing for us.'

'Sam,' she stared up at him, 'we've got to stop this! We've got to make them realise we're us!

'Let me talk to your dad!' Her long fingers were gripping his arms tightly. 'Let me try to explain. I've never even met him. He's only *seen* me! If he'll accept me, then maybe he'll get my mum to be reasonable.'

She fumbled with her train of thought. 'Nan isn't a problem. Not the same way. At least, I don't think she is. She started talking to me this afternoon, proper talking, I mean. I thought she was going to tell me everything. But she didn't.' The girl shrugged helplessly. 'All I know is, all I'm certain about is that this *isn't* to do with us, not completely! It's to do with something that's inside their heads, particularly Mum's, and I hate her!'

'Jodie, darling, don't.' He held her close, feeling her shaking against him. 'You don't mean that. She's your mother!'

'I don't care!' Her eyes met his squarely. 'I love *you*, Sam! I want to spend the rest of my life with you, not with her and all her silly rules and regulations and what's right and wrongs!

'I don't know about my dad.' She broke away from him and started walking briskly over the slippery ground. 'He was just a guy who was there and shouted at me a lot. I don't miss him, not the same way Pia does. I think maybe I never really liked him all that much. But that doesn't matter. And anyway,' she stopped and half turned, 'I've got a feeling at least *he'd* understand how we feel! I reckon it's the same way he felt about Mum once, and how she felt about him.

'Only,' she lowered her head and rubbed her hand under her nose, 'she's gone and got dried up! She's forgotten it all! She's forgotten what it's like, actually being properly in love!

'Please, Sam,' she stared at him and he felt himself beginning to struggle for survival in her eyes, 'let me talk to your dad. Please? Before any of us gets any more hurt.'

'All right.' There was nothing else he could say. Nothing else he could do in the face of so much pent-up determination. 'But what happens if that makes things worse?'

'How can they *get* any worse?' she asked bitterly. 'What else can they do to us? Shoot us like hurt horses?

This is supposed to be the season of goodwill on earth to all men or something! Hark the herald angels! The holly and the ivy!' Her voice rose hysterically. 'Love came down at Christmas!

'They're already keeping us apart. They're making us act like – like criminals. What more can they do? Send you away to college? OK, fine! Then I go away, too!

'Send me back to Gramps and Grandmom in Australia? OK, fine! But the minute I'm old enough I'll just come back and find you, if you haven't found me first!'

She gulped in a deep breath of cold air, then wrapped her arms round herself, hugging herself tight and rocking back and forward.

'When all this started,' she said finally in a more even voice, 'we were just a couple of kids who liked each other, right? But that isn't true any more, is it, Sam? *Is* it?' She looked at him fiercely and he shook his head.

'Then tomorrow afternoon I'm coming round to see your dad. I won't tell Mum, or Nan, or even Pia. I – I'll just say I'm going for a walk to think about my Christmas shopping or something. OK?' She moved towards him and touched his cheek gently.

'OK.' He nodded, caught her hand and kissed the back of the damp woollen glove.

'Right.' She smiled. 'Now I'd better go get Pia. With my luck the rehearsal will have stopped and she'll be having a snowball fight with every kid in the village!

'And Sam?' She leaned closer and kissed him, and he could feel the salt from her tears on her lips. 'I mean everything I've said. They can all go to hell, except you!'

Then she was gone, slipping through the trees away

from the stone like a tall determined ghost.

Sam watched until she was out of sight, then turned and headed for the other side of the wood.

An owl hooted plaintively. Nothing answered it, and it was only as he swung himself over the drystone wall into his own lane that he realised the snow had turned to rain, as if the sky was crying for them, too.

Chapter 11

It was easier than she'd imagined for Jodie to get out on her own the next afternoon.

Barbara Wright had been confined to bed, on doctor's orders, to rest her hip and Karen, in a sudden flurry of daughterly activity, had decided to make a Christmas cake as a surprise for her mother.

'For goodness' sake, Jodie, go for a walk or something!' she'd yelled, furiously creaming sugar and butter together in the old-fashioned china bowl. 'You're making me nervous hanging round the kitchen like this! And if you're in the village, buy some stamps at the post office, please. It's time we all sat down and wrote those cards Nan's bought.'

She'd gone up to her room, changed her sweater, then brushed her hair hard, screwing up her face at its reflection in the mirror.

'Gordon Miller's nice,' she'd kept telling herself as she'd queued at the post office counter in the shop for stamps. 'He's got to be nice,' she'd added as she'd plodded along the lane towards his house. 'He's Sam's dad, and Sam likes him. So I've got to like him, too. And *he's* got to like me!'

It had taken every inch of courage she possessed to knock on the door, but now she stood in the comfortably untidy kitchen, facing Gordon and reminding him of a vixen he'd once seen caught by a snare. The eyes were the same, defiant but frightened of being hurt any more at the same time.

Outside the winter garden dripped with rain, miserably grey and unwelcoming. Yesterday's snow had disappeared as rapidly as it had arrived, leaving a cloying unhappy dampness behind it.

He didn't know what to say to Jodie. It was too old and too well-kept a secret, but looking at her now appealing to him was like looking at Karen doing much the same thing all those years ago.

Suddenly Claire's face flashed across his memory. What would *she* have done? How would she have dealt with this?

Although the awful intensity of losing her wasn't as strong as it had been, he still missed her desperately. He missed her good common sense, her laugh, and her apparently endless patient ability to listen to other people.

'Mr Miller,' Jodie was twisting her hands in front of her, lacing and unlacing her long fingers, 'I know Sam didn't want me to come, but he feels so bad about having lied to you. I don't want him to feel bad about anything, and particularly not if I'm what's caused it.'

She was almost as tall as he was, Gordon suddenly realised as she looked him full in the face. 'I love him, and he loves me. We didn't mean it to happen like that. I'm sorry. We didn't set out to be anything more than friends.'

'Jodie,' Gordon sat down in Claire's old chair, 'you're both too young to know what love's all about. Do you honestly suppose that what you're feeling for each other could last a lifetime? D'you even think it could stand the test of a long separation, something like that?'

'It's standing that test already!' she flashed, then bit her lip. He watched her struggle to pull herself back under control.

'Mr Miller,' she was almost pleading and he felt his heart go out to her, 'we're not asking you to let us get engaged or married or anything like that. We're just asking you to let us be together without having to hide in corners all the time. Surely that makes sense?'

'Yes, I suppose it does, on one level anyway.' He rubbed his hand tiredly over his eyes then looked at her. 'Perhaps, if it were left to me, I'd just let you both get on with things. But it isn't my decision, Jodie, and I may as well warn you now that neither your mother nor your grandmother are likely to change their ideas one jot.'

'But *why*?' She perched on the edge of the wooden stool, as completely unhappy as only a sixteen-year-old can be. 'What's wrong with Sam? What happened? What's wrong with me?' A thought struck her, sped across her face registering horror. 'We — we're not related or something, are we?'

Despite himself, Gordon laughed, and the tension that had been closing in moved back to the corners of the room.

'No, you're not related in the slightest! That's the one thing I *can* promise you. Though,' he frowned suddenly, 'is there any reason why that should be more of a problem than all the other problems you seem to be having?'

'You mean, have we been to bed together?' The sentence was clipped, cold and far too direct. It made Gordon feel as if he were the child and she the adult in control.

He nodded, embarrassed.

'No, we haven't.' She faced him again. 'We're not like that, that's what I keep trying to tell you! We're not just out for a quick grope and a thrill! We really care about each other, Mr Miller.

'Maybe it isn't the kind of love that can last an entire lifetime. Neither of us knows for certain. How can we? We haven't had the chance. How can anybody? Did *you* know when you married Mrs Miller?' She paused, gulping for breath, then looked down at her hands, her face flushed in embarrassment.

'I'm sorry. I shouldn't have said that. It was rude and it's none of my business anyway. Sam told me what happened with your wife, a bit of it at least. It still hurts him, so it must hurt you even more.'

'Yes.' He blinked at the girl's perspicacity and suddenly wondered whether she'd ever been young, herself; whether she'd ever had what he and Claire would've considered a normal childhood, full of toys and day trips and birthday parties. Somehow he doubted it, though not because of Karen – Karen had a fierce protectiveness towards her two girls that had been born, he suspected, out of having to struggle with

86

them on her own for much longer than she should have.

'Forgive me?' Jodie said softly, leaning towards him a little, and he found himself nodding again.

Sam had told him, last night, she had squirrel eyes, and he saw what his son meant. They were large and vulnerable and very, very wary. But somewhere behind them there was a depth and strength that he found himself, at his age, envying.

He hesitated, beginning to wish that when Sam had announced this visit he hadn't insisted the boy stay out of the way. 'I loved Claire very much indeed.'

'*But never as much*', a particle of his mind screamed unfaithfully '*as I loved Karen Wright! When she told me she was leaving with Bob Mitchenson I seriously considered killing myself. I couldn't believe she could do that to me! I couldn't believe she would really go to Australia to live and I'd never see her again. But I just gave up. I couldn't fight her any more. And her mother was right. I was weak.*'

And if I was weak then, he thought unhappily, I mustn't be weak now. I mustn't let this child influence the decisions that have already been taken.

Does history, he wondered, really repeat itself? Does everything simply go round in circles until the same starting point is reached all over again?

He shook his head, shambled to his feet and crossed to the sideboard to pour himself a drink.

Jodie watched him anxiously.

One day, Sam would grow up to be like him. They were very similar. Both had the same attitude of puzzled gentleness, as if neither of them could work out really why they'd been put on this planet at all.

Gordon sipped his whisky, then cleared his throat and turned back to Jodie.

'All I can tell you about this entire – mess,' he waved his free hand at nothing helplessly, 'is what you already know, more or less.

'Before I met and married Claire I was in love with your mother, very deeply in love, if that doesn't sound too old-fashioned. For some reason,' he smiled deprecatingly, 'at that time *her* mother trusted her with me, probably because I'm so much older she thought I'd be a steadying influence.

'Your mother', he hesitated, searching for the best words, 'loved me too in her way, I think. But when your dad came along, that was it.' He snapped his fingers in a dismissive gesture. 'He threw stars and travellers' tales in her eyes, and because she wanted adventure and excitement, she took off with him.

'Unlike you and Sam, she and I *had* been to bed together, as you put it. We preferred to call it "making love". When she left me for Bob Mitchenson, I felt she'd cheapened us both. It wasn't a sensible concrete feeling.' He could sense Jodie about to interrupt and argue with him. 'When you're jilted, thrown over, ditched – whatever the current expression is – you're not sensible.

'Barbara Wright blamed me for everything that happened. She'd taken me into her confidence when Karen was just beginning to grow up, and she made me promise to respect that confidence – *and* to respect Karen.

'I've managed the first. I'm afraid I failed in the latter.

'Your mother walked out on *her* mother, Jodie,' he swallowed some more of the neat spirit, 'too soon after her father had died.

'She adored her dad, and she couldn't believe it when he simply wasn't around any more. Maybe that's one of the other things that happened with Bob Mitchenson – he offered her an escape route and she grabbed it.

'But he wasn't a particularly pleasant character. We found out, don't ask me how,' he frowned at her, 'that he'd already had one wife, and he'd been in trouble with the police since he'd come to Britain. Perhaps Karen thought she could reform him, I don't know. Certainly the marriage lasted a respectable time.

'But Barbara was terrified for her. I was frightened for us all because there didn't seem to be anything I could do.'

'I still don't understand,' the girl said slowly, 'what this has to do with Sam and me.

'Sure, I'm Bob Mitchenson's daughter – but I'm Karen's daughter, too. *And* Barbara's granddaughter!'

'And that', Gordon muttered under his breath, 'is most of the problem!'

Jodie looked at him curiously, head tilted to one side, one eyebrow half-raised.

'Forget what I said.' He crossed to the window and stared out. The rain had thickened to sleet, but the sky was clearing towards the west and there was a good chance of frost later.

'All right,' she agreed quietly. 'But please tell me why all this has to keep Sam and me apart. It's not just us who are hurting from it. Look at yourself!' She stood up quickly, clumsily, and the stool rocked backwards.

'Look at Mum! What good is it all doing?'

'Probably none,' he agreed. 'But it's the way things have to be at the moment, Jodie.

'I've made three promises in my life which I intend to stick by.

'One was to your grandmother. One was to Sam's mother, to look after him in the best possible way I could. And one was to myself. That one,' he turned towards her, feeling very old and very tired, 'was to make very sure I never interfered again in anyone else's life.

'So far,' he sighed, 'I've managed. I intend to go on managing. But if I were to agree to you and Sam meeting now, I'd be interfering in your mother's life and in what she wants for you. Can you understand that?'

'Yes.' The girl's eyes met his and seemed to stare straight through him. 'But I think you're wrong. I think you're breaking your promise to Sam's mum, because he loves me the same way I love him, and not letting him see me isn't looking after him in the best possible way.

'You're all —' her voice rose, for the first time showing signs of losing control — 'turning us into cheats because of the stupid things that happened years ago! Well,' she fastened her coat, fumbling — he noticed — with the bottom toggle as if she couldn't see it properly, 'I just hope you're right! Grown-ups are always supposed to be right, aren't they? But over the last two or three years I've discovered they aren't always. They just keep insisting they are!

'Thanks, Mr Miller,' she pushed her hand out towards him, 'for seeing me and talking to me at least. I appreciate that. But please don't expect *me* to give you any promises! I love Sam too much.'

Then with what sounded like a muffled sob she walked quickly across the uneven floor and went out, latching the door quietly behind her.

Gordon took a deep breath, followed by an even deeper swallow of whisky, and discovered, not entirely to his surprise, that he was shaking.

Of all the people in all the world he could have wished Sam to meet and fall in love with, he would only ever – now he'd met her – have wished for Jodie.

He walked slowly to the sideboard, slid open the top drawer, and pulled out Claire's photograph from the place where he kept it, underneath her best linen napkins.

'Oh Claire!' He looked at the laughing face. 'Why aren't you here? Why can't you just talk to me and tell me how to handle this mess?'

Sleet lashed the window viciously and the bare branches of the apple trees at the bottom of the garden ducked into the wind, twisting upwards like arms, he thought fancifully, crying out for help.

He refilled his glass, picked the battered address and telephone pad out of the empty wooden fruit bowl, and walked purposefully out into the hall.

Chapter 12

Jodie wandered miserably down the lane away from the house, shivering as the north-easterly wind cut through her.

Of all the people in the world she would have trusted to at least try to understand, Sam's father had headed the list.

'But he's just like everybody else!' she muttered into her collar. 'He won't take a chance on us. He's fenced in, like all England's little fields and towns!'

She brushed the sleet out of her eyes and stood for a second in the comparative shelter of the hedge, glancing at her watch and trying to decide whether to hang around to collect Pia from school, or to go straight home.

There wasn't a chance of seeing Sam, she knew that. His dad had explained that he'd gone into Sheffield for the day with some deliveries, and Jodie had guessed — correctly — that Gordon Miller hadn't wanted the extra hassle of having him around when Jodie appeared.

Maybe I should try to talk to Nan, she thought, splashing through a muddy puddle and watching a bedraggled wood pigeon shake out its feathers in one of the pine trees. Or maybe I should just give up and ask if I can go back to Australia.

She shrugged at herself impatiently. Going back to

Australia was just a stupid dream, and it wasn't one she particularly wanted to have come true anyway, even if the money for the fare had been available, which she knew it wasn't.

'There's got to be *some* way to straighten all this out,' she said aloud, short-cutting through the woods, past the stone, towards the village and home.

Strangely, particularly since Pia had started at school and Mum had been so busy with the seasonal shopping and arranging, she'd actually begun to think of the cottage as home, and she quickened her steps, looking forward to the warmth from the open fire and Edward's lazy, purring welcome.

All the lights were on at the front as she finally walked up the path, and she hesitated for a second, frowning.

Something in the way the cottage looked was wrong. It seemed to have straightened itself up, pulled itself in on itself tightly, like an old lady waiting for an argument.

She pushed open the door, pulled off her coat, shook it and hung it up on the rack with the others. There was a battered tweed hat perched there, with rain still glistening on its brim, and she shivered suddenly.

She'd seen that hat already that afternoon. It had been balanced on top of an abstract wooden carving in a corner of Gordon Miller's kitchen. She'd noticed it when she'd first gone in, because it had made the carving look as if it were wearing a drunken lampshade, and she'd wanted to giggle.

' . . . Karen, it could be we're being stupid.' The words were indistinct, but the voice was recognisably Gordon's. 'Your daughter's a very determined and persuasive young lady.'

Her mother's voice was icy. 'My daughter is still a little girl, at least emotionally. What on earth does she think she knows about being in love, Gordon? Please, be reasonable!'

Jodie stood where she was in the shadows of the coat rack. If a hurricane had suddenly hit the house she couldn't have moved. Her feet seemed to have sprouted roots that anchored her to the floor, and her arms and back felt stiff and heavy.

'What did *you* think you knew about being in love at her age, Karen?' Gordon's voice was just as icy, but more reasonably pitched.

'I thought I knew it all!' The retort was sharp. 'And I didn't, did I? That's why I don't want the same thing to happen to Jodie.'

'You can't stop her caring about someone, and believe me she *does* care. I think they both do.' Gordon's voice had softened and Jodie craned closer to the door to listen. 'Sam is walking round with a face that scrapes the ground all the time.

'He used to laugh a lot, like Claire. He used to make *me* laugh. He doesn't do either any more. Last night, when he told me he'd been seeing Jodie and that she was coming to visit me this afternoon, was the nearest thing I've seen to any kind of animation in his face for weeks.

'Karen,' there was a long, considered pause, 'I think we're wrong. What happened between you and me, that's over and done with. And it's our argument anyway, not theirs. I think we should give them a chance. I'll talk to your mother, try to explain how things have changed to her. She'll listen to me.'

'She may.' Jodie shivered at her mother's tone. 'I won't. I love my girls, Gordon. I want the best in the world for them. And I don't want either of them to make the same mistake I made with Bob. I can't take the chance that they'll ruin their lives the way I seem to have done.'

For a moment Jodie wondered if her mother was crying, and she moved forward slightly, trying to brace herself to walk into the room. Being a fly on the wall might have advantages, but not if you were the fly that was being talked about.

'All right.' Gordon Miller sounded resigned. 'But please don't blame me this time if it all goes wrong. Sam and Jodie are people, Karen. They aren't actually children any more. I realised that this afternoon.

'You never met Claire, did you?' He changed the subject abruptly and Jodie could imagine her mother shaking her head and sniffing.

'She was one of the most understanding people I'm ever likely to come across. She knew I'd married her on the rebound from you. And she knew, right up until the day she died, that I still cared about you in my way. But *she* loved *me* with the same kind of love I can see now in Jodie for Sam. It was a genuine, I'll-never-cheat love.'

'And mine wasn't, I suppose?' Karen's voice was very low, very hard.

'I don't know.' Gordon sounded helpless. 'I don't think either of us knew, and your mother wasn't a lot of help, was she?'

'No.' The word fell away miserably and Jodie felt a lump start at the back of her throat. 'But I'm still not prepared to change my mind, Gordon. I don't want them to see each other. You tackle Sam. I'll handle Jodie. And what I'd also very much like to know,' Jodie heard the chairs scrape back and the beginnings of movement towards the door, 'is just *how* they've managed to meet at all over the last few weeks.'

'That, I would have thought, was obvious.' Barbara Wright's voice cut in on the other two and Jodie began to feel physically sick. She wanted to turn and run back outside into the sleet. Wanted to go — anywhere. As long as it was far away from the cottage and the black, thickening atmosphere she could feel beginning to grow.

'What d'you mean, Mum? And what're you doing up, anyway?' she heard Karen ask stiffly.

'I'm up because I was sick to death of lying in bed. I came down about fifteen minutes ago to make a cup of tea, and then I heard voices.

'Good afternoon, Gordon.' Jodie could imagine her grandmother inclining her head regally towards Mr Miller, and could almost see him shuffle his feet, as uncomfortable as a schoolboy in the headmistress's study. 'We don't often have the pleasure of your company.'

'Mum, stop playing games!' Karen almost shouted impatiently. 'What's so obvious about how Jodie and Sam have been able to meet? What do you know that we don't?'

'I don't *know* anything.' Jodie heard her grandmother's skirts rustle as she settled into her favourite armchair close to the fire. 'I merely suspect that your younger daughter, Karen, may have been a party to all this. Pia is' — there was a hesitation followed by a

96

half-laugh – 'even more strong-willed than Jodie, if that's possible.

'And it may have escaped your notice, dear,' the last word was emphasised sarcastically and Jodie wriggled uncomfortably, 'but Pia actually adores her big sister. She'd do anything for the girl!

'Also,' Jodie had a sneaking suspicion her grandmother was thoroughly enjoying herself at Gordon and her own mother's expense, 'I find it difficult to believe that the tilting ground at Gawsworth Hall should be open to the public at all if it was quite as muddy as it appeared to be on the day Jodie took Pia there.

'I would strongly suspect Pia went in one direction, towards Nether Alderley and the Roberts, perhaps, while Jodie went in quite another.

'Of course,' this time a feather could've been heard dropping in the pause, 'I could be wrong. But somehow, I very much doubt it.'

Jodie's entire skin felt prickly and on fire. Her heart seemed to have moved from her chest to her throat and was beating so hard it threatened to choke her. Whatever muscles in her legs normally held them up had turned to jelly, and the urge to scream out loud was so strong she found she was actually biting hard into the back of her hand.

'Hey, sport!' The front door opened and Pia blew in in a flurry of dead leaves and rain. 'What's up? Why're you hiding behind the coat-rack?'

She dumped her school satchel in the centre of the floor, pulled off her raincoat and shook her head like a wet dog.

'I liked it more when it was snowing!' she grumbled crossly, standing on tiptoe to hang up the damp coat.

Then she looked at her sister properly for the first time, and colour seemed to drain from her face.

'Jodie, what is it? What's the matter?'

They stared at each other, then Jodie managed to nod towards the living-room.

'Nan,' she whispered in a strangled voice. 'She seems to know everything, including about you. And Sam's dad's here, too.'

'Oh.' Pia sat down on the bottom stair and matter-of-factly pulled off her wellingtons. 'Well, what do we do now?'

But before Jodie could answer, the living-room door swung open and Karen Mitchenson stood there, white-faced and shaking.

Chapter 13

The swirling five-dimensional row that followed was the worst experience of Jodie's life.

Their mother had never hit either of them before, but she strode across the hall, pulled Pia roughly to her feet and slapped her face hard.

'How *dare* you!' she hissed, while the younger girl stood there, her own face as white as Karen's apart from the red mark beginning to flare angrily on her cheek. 'I thought I'd brought you both up to behave decently and sensibly! Obviously I was wrong. Obviously your father had much more influence over you than I ever realised. Get upstairs now, Pia, and stay in your room. It makes me sick to even look at you!

'And as for you, madam,' she whirled round on Jodie, her original pallor giving way to a blotchy high colour, 'if one quarter of what I've heard or what your grandmother suspects is true, you may as well know I'll never trust you again! In fact,' she seemed to sag, 'I'll never want to see you again.

'You've let me down, both of you!' Her voice was almost out of control. 'You've behaved like stupid, selfish little children, and you both deserve a good beating!'

'Steady on, Karen.' Gordon Miller stood in the doorway, frowning at the immobile little scene in front of him. 'As I've already tried to point out, it isn't entirely their faults. We haven't exactly bothered to listen to them much, or hear their side of things. And we aren't,' he put his hand reassuringly on Karen's arm, but she shrugged him impatiently away, 'living in a Victorian age any more. We can't just lock them away and forget about them.'

'Unfortunately!' Karen spat, then turned to Pia, who was shivering on the stairs.

'Go to your room *now*,' she said in a slightly more controlled voice. 'Your grandmother and I will decide what to do with you once we've talked to your sister. But I warn you, Pia,' the words spun threateningly through the dusty electric light of the hall, 'you can forget all about your outings to the Roberts, or anyone else you happen to know.

'From now on, *I* shall take you to school, and collect

you from it every day. Any freedom of action you may have thought you brought with you from Australia can be put to the back of your head. I want to know, from this second onwards, precisely *what* you're doing, when you're doing it, and even *why* – every second of the day. Is that clear?'

Pia nodded dumbly, all the fight and determination draining out of her. Then she walked forward, picked up her school satchel, and without looking back at anyone plodded miserably up the narrow stairs.

'Mum, please!' Jodie's voice was shaking but she couldn't help herself. 'This isn't Pia's fault! Don't take it out on her. She was just doing what I asked because she thought it was a bit of a giggle. Leave her alone. Don't just grab all her friends away from her like this. It isn't right.'

'Neither are you!' Karen stalked angrily back to the front room door, threw it fully open and gestured for Jodie to follow her. 'In all my life I'd never have believed you could behave like this!

'What's so special about Sam Miller? Has he woven some kind of ridiculous spell round you or something?'

'Maybe,' Jodie agreed, following her slowly, desperately trying to avoid the look of compassion she knew was in Gordon's face. 'Or maybe you've just turned old-fashioned and strait-laced, Mum! You've been different,' she added, with a quick flash of insight, 'ever since we've been in England. It's almost like' – she looked round helplessly, fighting back tears – 'you feel you've got to use us to prove something to Nan!'

'Don't speak to your mother like that!' Barbara Wright's words were sharp but her voice had, Jodie realised, a slightly warmer edge to it. 'Simply tell us all, please, why you expressly went against our wishes and continued to see Sam? You lied, and you cheated. Why?'

'Because I love him,' she answered simply, body sagging forward. 'I – I couldn't just give him up for what seemed like a whole load of stupid reasons. And I've gone around with enough other guys to actually *know* how I'm feeling! We need each other. Why can't you try to believe me?'

She slumped down suddenly on the edge of the sofa and put her head in her hands.

'OK, what we did was wrong. We shouldn't have used Pia so we could meet. But neither Pia nor I ever told you a *downright* lie. We always just – well, bent the truth a bit, I guess. And,' she looked up at Gordon Miller, who was standing fiddling with his hat, 'if it hadn't been for the fact that *Sam* had to lie to his dad and felt rotten about it, chances are you still wouldn't know what had been happening.

'Only,' her face softened, 'Sam was sick with himself for lying, and I was sick with both of us. That's why I went to see Mr Miller. That's why I tried to explain everything to him.' A bitter little smile quirked up her mouth at one corner. 'At least he *did* bother to listen to me.'

She stared down at her long fingers, then suddenly clenched them into fists. 'Sam and I aren't doing anything really wrong. Neither of us is a criminal, and we're not Romeo and Juliet, either! But we can't help how we feel about each other, and it's all just made a lot worse because you've forced us to hide away all the time.'

A sudden gust of wind blew smoke from the fire out

into the room, and Jodie glanced sadly towards the window.

It was snowing again. Large, picture-book flakes were tossed against the glass, then melted slowly, trickling down to the sill in spattered patterns.

A few early Christmas cards on the mantelpiece rustled in the draught. A log hissed and spat into blue-yellow flame. Edward snored on his cushion, oblivious to the drama going on around him, and Jodie suddenly found herself listening to the rest of the silence inside the room and wondering how Pia was.

'Gordon,' Barbara Wright was the first person to break it, clearing her throat uneasily, 'how do you feel about all this?'

'Unhappy.' The man shrugged. 'And helpless. But I made you a promise Barbara. I've never broken it. I don't intend to now.

'However, I would advise,' he crammed his hat on to his head and fastened his jacket, 'that *you* talk to your daughter. History, in this family at least, seems to have a habit of repeating itself, and I have the strangest feeling nothing any of us do will make much more difference this time than it ever has in the past.

'Goodbye, Karen.' He glanced towards Jodie's mother, who was huddled into an armchair. 'If I were you, I'd think over one or two of the things Jodie's said and honestly believes. You might well learn from them.

'Goodbye, Barbara. A very happy Christmas, when it eventually arrives.

'And Jodie,' he moved towards the girl and touched her lightly on the shoulder, 'I'll tell Sam what's happened. Don't worry about that. I wish I'd been able to make things better for you both, but apparently I can't.

I'm sorry.'

She stared up at him, her enormous eyes cloudy with tears. Then she smiled suddenly and gripped his hand.

'I know,' she whispered softly. 'Thank you for trying. I – I didn't actually expect it to work. I didn't even expect you to do it. Will you give Sam a message?'

He nodded slowly, wanting to cradle her in his arms and hug away all the hurt, the way he had done with his son so many times when he'd been small and frightened and out of his depth.

'Just tell him I feel the same. Tell him nothing's going to change that. I'll be eighteen in a year and ten months. It isn't so long to wait. Tell him that, too, please!'

Her hand fell away, back down to her lap like a dead bird, and Gordon massaged her shoulder gently. Then without another word he turned and walked out of the room.

Barbara Wright sighed as she heard the front door slam and felt the swirl of cold air that had come into the hall with Gordon's exit.

His remark about history repeating itself had struck far too close to home, and for the first time in over eighteen years she found herself missing Bill Wright with an intensity that almost made her gasp aloud.

'I think, Jodie,' she said in a low voice, 'before any of this goes any further, we could all use a cup of tea. Would you make one, please? And take one up to Pia. There's no reason for the child to starve simply because she's in disgrace.'

Then she turned to her daughter and eyed her almost distastefully, Jodie thought, as she crept out of the room.

'Karen,' she heard her grandmother say as she began to close the connecting door to the kitchen behind her, 'we are all being utterly ridiculous and considerably more childish than the children. There's something I want to tell you now, and I want you to listen to me very carefully indeed, with absolutely no interruptions.'

Jodie shut the door quietly, crossed to the kettle, and then stood for a second staring out at the blizzard-blown back garden, shivering and hugging herself. The snow had thickened dramatically. The vegetable patch and the lawn were already covered in white and the Brussels sprout plants loomed in the half-light like cousins of E. T., who all wanted to call home.

What am I going to do, she wondered, throwing away the cold tea from the pot and scooping the soggy leaves on to a piece of kitchen paper. What *can* I do? What can anybody do?

She leaned her head against the glass of the window and closed her eyes.

A jagged, barely connected strip of memories flashed towards her, like someone using the fast-forward button on a video recorder.

Christmas in Australia – Pia, aged eight, laughing excitedly and pulling at the wrapping paper on her presents. They hadn't had a tree that year because it had been their first year in Sydney with their other grandparents.

Then Pia's face, dissolving into a black frown because there had been nothing – not even a card – from their dad.

Jodie, before the massive turkey-and-trimmings evening meal carefully laid out on the veranda, grabbing the little girl by the hand and begging to be allowed to take her down to the beach for a quick swim, just to cheer her up.

Pia, careering through the surf with other kids her own age, yelling, 'Merry Christmas, everybody!' at the top of her voice while Jodie watched, smiling, from her place on the hot sand.

It was all very different and seemed a very long time ago and very far away from the way things were now.

Pia boasting on the plane to a slightly older boy that she was an Aussie, of course, not a stupid Pommie like him.

Pia at Heathrow. Pia on the shuttle to Manchester. Pia bubbling with an excitement that had eventually transferred itself to Karen and herself.

Now she straightened slowly, remembering the shock and pain on her sister's face when Karen had slapped her, because of what she, Jodie, had done and because of the selfish way she'd behaved because of Sam. Pia was going to be made to suffer for something that wasn't in any way her responsibility.

She fumbled in the fridge, pulled out a jar of peanut butter, then cut some chunks from the loaf of new bread her mother must have bought in the village, and knifed on the spread lavishly.

She made the tea, poured some into a mug for her sister, then picked up mug and plate and tiptoed as quietly as she could into the hall.

For once, the stairs didn't creak, and she eased open the bedroom door gently, some of the tea spilling over the side of the mug and on to the worn carpet.

The room was in darkness and felt bitterly cold, but Jodie could just make out a small humped shape in

Pia's bed with the duvet and heavy bedspread apparently pulled up over its head.

'Pia,' she whispered softly, groping with her elbows to find the dressing-table so she could put the plates down. 'I've brought you some tea. Nan said I should. And I made you a sandwich. OK?'

There was no answer.

'Come on, Pia.' She settled everything carefully beside her hairbrush then fumbled in the darkness for the light switch. 'Stop kidding around. It's only me.'

The cold glow from the blue-fringed shade flooded the room and Jodie blinked, then frowned, rubbing her arms and crossing quickly to close the wide-open window.

A flurry of snow hit her in the face as she eased it down, and the wind round the cottage had changed its voice from a low threatening moan to a high-pitched keening whine.

'Pia?' She sat on the edge of the bed and touched the motionless hump. 'I'm sorry. I'm sorry about everything. I'll make it up to you somehow.

'I,' she hesitated then gulped, 'I'm not going to see Sam again. Not after this. Not after the way Mum went on at you. None of it's your fault. Now come on. Drink your tea. I can't stay up here too long. They'll just come looking for me. And –' she tried to put a smile in her voice '– it's snowing again. Real heavy this time.'

The hump didn't move, didn't appear to be breathing, and a kind of cold gulping dread gripped Jodie.

'Pia?' She pulled back the bedspread.

Two pillows, plumped into a half-curve, filled the space where her sister should have been.

'*Pia*!' She bit back the shout, leaping to her feet and

beginning frantically to search the room.

Pia's school uniform had been dropped in a pile and kicked into the corner formed by the side of the wardrobe and the sloping eaves wall.

Her old anorak was gone from its peg on the back of the door and, Jodie realised helplessly, beginning to shake and feel sick again, the small worn toy koala bear she'd had since she was a baby had disappeared as well.

'No! Oh please, no!' she breathed, scrabbling with the pillows on the bed, searching frantically for a note or any other clue that might tell her where the girl had gone.

Wind and snow drove against the window, rattling the panes. It was pitch-dark outside. If she'd gone out, wearing just her anorak and jeans . . . !

Jodie shuddered.

And how *long* had she been gone, anyway? How long had everything downstairs actually taken? It had felt like for ever and must, she reckoned, have been close on an hour if you included the conversation with Nan and her own daydreaming in the kitchen.

She got up. Yanked open drawers. Slammed them closed again. Then some sixth sense made her stop in front of the copy of *The Wind in The Willows* on her own bedside table.

She opened it, hands shaking, and a hastily-printed note torn from an exercise book dropped out.

'*I took the rose,*' it said, blotched with tears, '*in case they found it. Don't worry. It'll be safe under the stone and that way you won't lose it, too. I'm not staying any more. I just can't. Tell them I'm sorry but I don't care what I did.*'

The 'Pia' was signed very large and very carefully and there were four kisses underneath it, heavily indented into the paper as if she'd held the pen in her fist and tried to put everything else she was feeling into those uneven crosses.

Jodie stared at it, her own tears joining the ones that had already formed blurred bumps on the pale blue lines.

Then carrying it carefully, she crossed the bedroom, opened the door and walked shakily downstairs.

'Mum. Nan.' She hesitated, blinking in the suddenly unfamiliar warmth of the main room. 'I think you'd better look at this.'

She held the paper towards her mother.

'Pia seems' – the room was spinning, its walls doing a crazy dance towards her and she blinked again, feeling completely empty – 'to have run away.'

Chapter 14

The silence stretched for ever.

Karen Mitchenson sat, staring at her elder daughter, hearing the words she'd just spoken but feeling completely incapable of understanding them.

For a reason she couldn't explain a nervous rush of laughter threatened to choke her.

Somehow, somewhere in her innermost mind, she'd been half-prepared for a running-away. But she had always pictured a *Wuthering Heights* scene with Jodie and young lover Sam running across the moors through drifting mist until they eventually found their own small patch of perfect sunlight.

She'd never once imagined it could be Pia – small, square, determined Pia with her ten-year-old unset face and occasional air of puzzlement – who'd take off into the storm.

She half-turned and looked towards the window.

Drifts of snow were already building up in uneven triangles at corners of the glass. The wind rattled in the chimney like a demented animal, and she shuddered.

'Give me that.' Barbara Wright's voice sounded unnaturally loud, even to herself. 'Where did you find it?'

'Upstairs. She – she must've climbed through the window. She always said that one day the ivy and wisteria would make a good escape route. She's changed her things.' Jodie clutched the back of a chair, the knuckles on her long hands white with tension. 'Her school clothes are kicked into a corner by the wardrobe. And her anorak's gone.

'Mum?' She appealed to Karen. 'What're we going to do? She'll *die* out there! And it's all my fault!'

'Don't be ridiculous!' Barbara snapped. 'Go and get the telephone pad by the phone in the hall. We've got to call the police immediately.'

'No!' Karen glared at her mother. 'No police. Not yet. She – she's probably only hiding in the garden or somewhere! Playing games. We've got to start searching for her. And when I find her,' she scrambled to her feet unsteadily. 'I'll thrash the living daylights out of her!'

'Karen, try not to be absurd!' Mother stared down

daughter while Jodie shuffled, trying to block out their voices: trying to concentrate on Pia and where she might've actually gone. 'We're in the middle of a storm. A *bad* storm. We could be without electricity at any minute, or hadn't you noticed the way the lights have been flickering? If the wind stays the way it is,' she glanced towards the white darkness outside, 'we'll be cut off. There'll be drifts feet high. Jodie's right.' She breathed in deeply. 'Pia could die unless we do something now!'

The room, Jodie thought, stood poised. Waiting.

Then a sudden knock on the front door broke the unholy silence.

'Someone's found her!' Karen whirled round. 'They've brought her back! A neighbour, maybe? Or one of her teachers!'

'Answer it, Jodie! Go on! Quickly!'

Jodie trailed across the worn carpet, mentally shaking her head. It was too easy an answer; too convenient an ending – and she knew Pia.

Pia wouldn't *let* herself be found. Couldn't they understand that? The note made it very clear, and the blotches on the paper showed she hadn't made up her mind to go just to frighten everybody. She'd meant what she'd written.

She shivered at the sudden change of temperature in the hall, then reluctantly opened the front door, concentrating on the snow swirling like dust across the mat.

'Jodie?' Sam stood there, bundled into an old army combat jacket and scarf, his cheeks and nose lashed red and glistening from the weather, his eyes frowning at her as if he didn't understand anything any more than she did.

'Sam?' She whispered the word in total disbelief. 'What're you doing here? Why've you come?'

He shrugged and snowflakes dripped to melting ice on his scarf. 'I talked to Dad. Then I went for a walk. To the stone. I was going to leave you a note. To tell you I still loved you, too. Then I found this.' He held out a coffin of damp tissue paper and Jodie took it from him gently, easing the sticky bits that were already beginning to tear away from the faded rose.

'I didn't know why it was there.' A kind of hurt Jodie had never seen before showed on his face and she took a half-step towards him, then stopped, swallowing hard, remembering that it was because of Sam and herself that Pia had disappeared. 'I thought maybe you hadn't meant your message to Dad. I thought maybe you'd slipped out and left the rose because you didn't want to see me again.'

'Oh Sam!' She launched herself forward then and hugged him. 'Oh no! It wasn't that! It couldn't ever be that! I didn't put the rose there. It . . .' She brushed the tears out of her eyes and frowned. 'It was Pia.

'She – she's run away. I just found her note. She said she'd taken the rose! But if she went to the stone, maybe she's still in the wood!

'Sam, we've got to go and get her! She's only wearing that old anorak she brought from Australia!' She shook him excitedly, knowing she couldn't be making a lot of sense but trusting him to understand.

'Jodie?' Her grandmother's shadow shifted across the two of them. 'Jodie, who *is* at the door?'

'It's me, Mrs Wright. May I come in?' Sam's arm was closely round Jodie's shoulders, giving her strength, holding her up mentally as well as physically. 'Jodie's told me about Pia. Have you called the police?'

'Not yet.' Barbara leaned heavily on her stick and frowned. Sam Miller might have been Gordon's twin at the same age. Underneath the apparent day-dreaming gentleness there was a strength that Barbara remembered all too clearly. 'And as you are here, you had better come in. For goodness' sake close that door, Jodie! It won't help Pia if *we* all catch pneumonia!'

She walked painfully to the three-legged table under the small round window, picked up the worn leather telephone pad and gestured impatiently for the two to go through to the main room.

The storm, she estimated, was almost at its height. The wind had a dying note to it. But when the wind went, she shuddered, the frost would come down. The snow would freeze. Fresh snow would fall on top of it. Then that would freeze, too. And for one small girl who had never known the intense cold of a bad British winter, there would be very little chance.

Sooner or later her legs would begin to hurt trying to plough through the drifts that, if Barbara was any judge, were already blown taller than she was in places. Her hands, unless she was wearing gloves – which her grandmother personally doubted – would turn from harsh red, to white, and then to a numbed blue-grey. She'd actually stop feeling cold. She'd laugh to herself and imagine she'd beaten the storm. Then she'd settle down in some piece of shelter somewhere, count the snowflakes, and – as Jodie had said – die.

It happened all the time in the mountains and on the

moors. Exposure. Hypothermia. Experienced climbers who knew about storms got caught out. Every year there were reports. Every year rescue teams risked their own lives. And every year, bodies were brought back.

She slammed the leather pad on to a side-table and glared at her own daughter, who was staring at Sam and Jodie as if they'd just landed from Mars.

'Karen?' Her voice sounded much firmer than she felt. 'This is the number. Call it now. The police will do everything they can, and they'll alert the emergency services.'

'No!' Karen turned towards her slowly, like someone in a daze. 'No police. Not yet. Let's go out and look. I don't want to involve the police. It's my fault she ran away. I hit her! They'll blame me! They're bound to blame me! And she's small. She can't have gone far. She'll be all right!'

'Karen!' Jodie and Sam watched in terrified fascination as Barbara's hand swung out and slapped Karen fiercely across the face. 'Pull yourself together! This isn't some silly television soap-opera you're watching! And this certainly isn't Australia! The police aren't going to blame you. Why should they? The only person who's blaming you is yourself!

'We have to find Pia. And we have to find her now!'

'Nan's right, Mum!' Jodie's voice shook. 'Nothing else matters. And she really could die out there while we're all arguing. We've got to *do* something!

'Sam?' She frowned at him, clutching his soaked jacket. 'Let's go? Now! We can try the wood. If she's been to the stone . . .?'

She trailed off helplessly. Sam's face seemed to have masked itself from her, as if he was scared of showing how he felt; rather the same way his father had looked, she thought wildly, when he'd begun to talk about his wife.

'The police!' Barbara interrupted, pushing the phone pad under Karen's nose. 'For once, do what you *know* is the sensible thing! Please!' She breathed in heavily. 'I happen to quite like both my grand-daughters. And I utterly *dislike*,' she emphasised the word, 'unnecessary funerals.'

'Mum!' Karen's body collapsed forward, hands cupping her mouth as if she wanted to stop herself screaming. 'Please . . .!'

'Oh for God's sake!' Sam moved quickly and easily away from Jodie. 'This is crazy!

'Jodie, get your coat and wellies. Wrap up really warm and try to find a torch if your nan has one. I'm going to ring Dad. The roads wil! be closed soon, but maybe if he puts the chains on he can get over here now in the car.

'And Mrs Mitchenson,' he spun round, eyeing the sobbing Karen distastefully, 'when he arrives, do your-self a very big favour and trust him this time, will you? Because after everything, even after Mum,' his voice softened, 'he only really cares about *you*.'

He pulled open the door, strode into the hall and then shouted back over his shoulder, 'Jodie, come *on*!' 'Where?' By the time he'd made the quick telephone call to Gordon, Jodie was ready, pushing the torch that Nan gave her into his pocket and carefully clutching a smaller spare one herself. 'Where do we start?'

He opened the door. The wind had dropped. Snow drifted lazily down from a clearing sky like a

114

haphazard net curtain someone had carelessly left lying around.

'Where?' she repeated, feeling his hand clutch hers comfortingly.

'The Edge, of course. Where else?' He bent and kissed her lightly. 'She took the rose and left it for us. There were footsteps going away through the wood, but I couldn't tell whose because the snow was blowing over them.

'She hasn't left *you*, Jodie.' His grip tightened as they negotiated the totally obscured front path. 'She'll have gone to somewhere she knows, and somewhere she knows *you* were happy in. Or at least,' he glanced at her anxiously, 'that's what I'm banking on. OK?'

She lifted her face. Blinked the snow away from it. Then smiled.

'OK.'

Chapter 15

'What happened?' The drifts in the lane were deeper than Jodie had anticipated and she waded along beside Sam, slipping and sliding, feeling unfamiliar muscles stress, grateful that he was there. 'I mean, between you and your dad?'

'I got back from Sheffield. He told me you'd been round. He told me,' he gripped her tightly, 'that he was impressed enough by you to go and talk to Karen. Then,' he hesitated, 'he told me one or two other things as well. I don't think he enjoyed doing it. It was all part of a promise he'd made to your nan.' He stopped, balancing on the uneven ground, and pulled Jodie closer to him. 'But he's on our side, Jodie. Your mum, well . . . ' He kissed her face lightly, smoothing the clinging dampness away from her hair. 'Maybe she knows, too. Maybe she doesn't. I've just about given up trying to work it all out!'

'Work *what* out? *Knows* what?' Jodie felt as if she were screaming inside. The snowflakes were drifting to a stop and far above the trees she could see the sky darken into deep sparkling blue pricked out with tiny pinpoints of stars. Everywhere was quiet and her voice sounded as if it was echoing off the bending firs.

'Your nan,' they plodded forward slowly, '*had* to marry your grandad. In other words, she was pregnant. But then she lost the baby.

'Your grandad was apparently a bit of a lad, a sailor with a girl in every port. That sort of thing. After a couple of bad years your nan finally found out she was having your mum and your grandad swore he'd give up all his wild ways, come out of the navy, settle down, make a life for them all – and make sure his little girl had the best life she could ever possibly have.

'That's what he did. But your mum must've been more like her dad than anybody realised, because when she was sixteen – same age as you, funny face,' he hugged her again, 'she was a sort of a tearaway, too.'

He helped her carefully over the gate on to the hidden path along to the Edge. 'My dad, as much as I understand it anyway, fell in love with her, although he

116

was eight years older than she was. Your nan trusted him, and dad never did anything to betray that trust.'

'You know what I mean?' He shifted uneasily, staring round, searching for tracks, for any sign of Pia.

'I think so,' Jodie murmured. 'But I don't understand.'

'Mrs Wright was frightened. She was frightened for your mum in case she got herself into the same bother as *she'd* done and wound up having to get married. She was frightened for your grandad, in case he ever found out that his darling little girl wasn't quite as innocent as he kept thinking. So she sort of handed over your mum to my dad to look after. It was a stupid thing to do, but then parents seem to get a bit stupid sometimes, don't they?'

A light wind rustled the bushes and soft snow dropped to the ground. There was no moon, but everywhere glowed with a brightness that Jodie found hurt her eyes.

'But why us? Why did it all have to get taken out on us?' She stumbled after him blindly, hardly feeling the wet sticks of trees brush at her face.

'Because when your *dad* came along, your nan blamed my dad for not being strong enough to keep them apart. Your grandad had just died, and she thought it was because he'd begun to guess what his daughter was really like and it had broken his heart.'

'What *was* she really like? She wasn't bad? Not properly, surely?' A large heavy lump seemed to have settled in Jodie's stomach and she almost dreaded his answer.

'No, of course not! Don't be daft!' He laughed. 'She was just having a good time. But it was the "Swinging

Sixties" – whatever that means – and all the papers were full of reports of drugs and teenage runaways, and God knows what else! Your nan didn't understand the change. She just knew what had happened to *her*, and she didn't want it to happen to your mum.

'When something a lot worse happened, when your mum ran off with your dad, your grandmother' (he swung himself clumsily down the hillside towards the place where they'd lain in the damp bracken and where Jodie had told him she never wanted him to be lonely again) 'blamed *my* dad. And she told him why she blamed him, but she made him promise he'd never repeat it all to anyone else. Then she never spoke to him again until this afternoon.'

'Sam,' Jodie's arm hung limply by her sides, 'that makes sense for *Nan*. But Mum? Why should Mum have tried to keep us apart?'

'I don't know.' He shook his head, bending forward to duck under the low, heavily snow-laden tree branches. 'Dad doesn't, either.

'Come on.' He felt behind him for her hand. Pulled her with him. 'The temperature's dropping. It's beginning to freeze. We've got to find Pia.'

And suddenly they saw her.

She was tucked into her anorak under the same tree where the squirrel had buried its nuts for the winter. A fine powdering of snow covered her hair and her shoulders. Her knees were hugged to her chest, her head bent forward, and in a strange strangled little voice she was singing, '*Of all the trees that are in the wood, the holly bears the crown.*'

'Pia!' Jodie started forward, slipping and sliding through the snow, gashing its immaculate whiteness so that leaves and brambles and bedraggled bracken suddenly sprung up round her as if they'd been startled out of their sleep.

'Hi, Jodie.' She opened one eye and smiled happily and peacefully. 'What're you doing here? Isn't it nice and quiet? I think this is the only time I've been warm since we came to England!'

Then the eye closed again, the long lashes fluttering gently against her cheeks.

'Pia!' Jodie grabbed her hands, trying to rub feeling into them. 'Pia, come on! Wake up! We're going home. Everything's all right! Everything's fine now!' She put her arms round the girl, rocking her back and forwards. 'Sam's here. That's how I found you. Please, Pia! Oh, *please*!' She sobbed the last word into her sister's soaking hair, then she looked up hopelessly at Sam. 'What's the matter with her? Why won't she talk to me?'

'Because she's unconscious, Jodie.' The older, heavier voice sliced the stillness and somewhere, far away in the valley, an owl hooted eerily. 'It's OK. Let her go. I'll take her. I'll carry her.'

Gordon Miller knelt in the snow, gently prising Jodie's fingers apart, and as gently starting to wrap the heavy travelling rug he'd brought round Pia's still figure.

'Dad?' Sam sounded as confused and astonished as Jodie felt. 'I thought you were going to the cottage! What're you doing here? How did you know . . .?'

'Where to find you all?' Gordon straightened slowly, hugging the bundle that was Pia to him. 'Instinct. Memory. I'm not sure which.

'It's where Karen and I used to come. And your

119

mother and me, too. I heard her talking to you about this place once, a long time ago. You probably don't even consciously remember that, yourself.

'But I had a feeling, just a feeling, that if there were going to be any more coincidences, they'd probably all coincide here. Like paths crossing. Or the seventh wave,' he glanced at Jodie and smiled reassuringly, 'the strongest surfer's wave of all. It's the one that always goes back to the sea.

'You and Sam, and now Pia, it all seems part of the same pattern. Part of the stony limits that can't ever hold love out, if either of you remember your Shakespeare.

'Now come on,' he started forward carefully, and Pia gave a little half-wriggle, 'let's get this runaway home. Everything else can wait' – he silenced his son with a look – 'until she's safely tucked up in bed.'

They crossed back along the Edge in complete silence, Gordon with Pia leading the way and Jodie, clinging desperately to Sam, following as the whispering snow started to gossip round them again.

Chapter 16

The rest of the evening and most of the night were a confusing muddle as far as Jodie was concerned. Everything had gone past in a whirling, tumbling kaleidoscope, and very little of it had made any sense.

She stretched luxuriously, blinking away from the unnaturally bright white light flooding through the window, and glanced at Pia's bed.

Her sister lay there, humped into a real half-circle this time, the still-soggy koala that she'd refused to be parted from propped up on the pillow next to her face.

The room was warm. Nan had insisted on turning up the central heating after they'd all got back. And, Jodie grinned to herself, there had been tears on her face when Gordon Miller walked through the cottage door with the shrouded Pia in his arms.

'Thank the Lord!' She could hear her grandmother's voice now. 'Thank God, Gordon! Where?'

'The Edge. The old place.' Sam's dad carefully laid Pia down on the battered sofa. 'You'd better call Dr Stevens. He'll be able to get here if he hurries. But it's snowing again. Tell him he'll need to use chains to get up the hill.'

'The old place.' Barbara Wright straightened and suddenly laughed, a very true, clear, young laugh, Jodie thought. 'Of course. Why not?

'Jodie. Sam.' She'd turned to the pair of them. 'Go and get dried off and changed. There are some things of your grandfather's, Jodie, in the bottom drawer of my wardrobe. Give them to Sam, before you both catch your deaths.

'Karen,' the voice was sharp, defying anyone to contradict it, 'take Gordon into the kitchen. Make some tea. There's whisky in the sideboard. I'll call the doctor. And to think,' as Jodie led Sam silently out, both of them bewildered by the sudden shifting lift of atmosphere, 'it'll soon be Christmas, too!'

Jodie showed Sam the bathroom, pulled the best and

fluffiest towels out of the airing cupboard and threw them through the door at him, then wandered into her grandmother's room, hardly realising she was still soaked to the skin herself. All that mattered was that Pia was safe, and that Sam had been allowed into the house. It was just a toehold on the ladder, but where a toe could grip, an entire foot could follow.

She opened the heavy mahogany wardrobe to expose the two built-in drawers at the bottom; she had pulled them open, coughing and beginning to sneeze at the smell of mothballs and lavender, and then carefully unfolded a pair of ancient grey trousers, a Viyella checked shirt, and a blue pullover.

No one had disturbed them for how many years, she wondered as she smoothed the creases out of the matted wool of the pullover.

Grandad's.

She hugged the sweater to her, then abruptly shook her head, thinking of Sam in the bathroom shivering, needing the clothes. Needing (she scrabbled at the drawer desperately) socks to warm his feet. Poor feet. Poor cold, tired feet.

Her hands picked up the book, almost without realising what it was, and she put it on the floor impatiently, pushing it to one side, needing the socks much more. For Sam. For shivering cold Sam, stuck in the bathroom with nothing but the fluffy towels for company . . .

'So she still kept it, even after all these years!' Her mother's voice was soft and faintly surprised. 'I didn't know. I didn't think it would still exist.'

'Mum?' She straightened back to her heels, a pair of patched grey socks in her hands.

'This.' Karen Mitchenson knelt on the floor in the muddle of clothing, holding the red exercise book and smiling down at it with a tired, faraway smile. 'I knew about it, you see. That's been the whole problem.'

'Oh.' Jodie scrambled to her feet, not at all sure she could trust her mother any more. Not at all sure that this woman, suddenly so much shorter and older and more wrinkled than she'd ever realised, was actually anything to do with her.

'Take the clothes to Sam, Jodie. Then come back here for a minute. Please?'

'Yes. Yes, of course.'

She hurried out of the room with its strangely narrow, high-headboarded double bed; knocked on the bathroom door; pushed the old faded trousers and shirt and pullover and darned socks through and heard Sam say, 'Jodie? I still love you.'

'I love you, too. Stony limits. Seventh waves. They won't stop that. Never!' Her voice, she thought, was far too young to be saying these words, but every part of her knew she meant them – and always would.

She moved on to her side, reaching her hand towards the table and the faded rose.

They'd taken it out of its tissue coffin eventually, she and her mother. They'd laid it gently and carefully on to the worn, almost colourless velvet of an empty jewellery box that Barbara Wright had brought.

Pia had watched, bright-eyed and pink-faced, and then Barbara had stooped, kissed all three of them in turn, and hurried as quickly as her bad hip would allow her from the room.

She'd paused in the doorway, ignored the sisters,

and looked directly at Karen.

'Maybe this time?' she'd murmured.

'Maybe,' her mother had agreed with a catch in her voice.

'Then tell them your truth, Karen. You owe them that. Gordon and Sam are staying here tonight. The snow's too thick. It's not safe to travel. Sam's in the little room. Gordon's taking the sofa. I think you should all talk, he and you especially.

'And Jodie? Pia?' She'd bobbed her head in a gesture that had reminded Jodie of a budgerigar she'd once sat watching back on the farm. 'It's almost Christmas. We must go shopping. Buy a tree.' She'd waved her arm vaguely. 'Decorate it. Have a proper white Christmas. I love you both.'

Then the door had closed and Karen had fussed with tucking in Pia, making sure she was warm enough, making sure she'd taken the tablets and the linctus Dr Stevens had pulled out of his ancient black briefcase after he'd thoroughly examined her.

Mother and daughter had faced each other across the shadowy room, with the snow still flickering and hissing occasionally outside.

'Why, Mum? Why did it all happen?' Jodie had clutched at the duvet cover, thinking about Australia, and the warmth – and the day her father had walked away, telling her not to be a dreamer all her life.

'Because of the book.' Karen's voice had sounded husky and she'd faced away from Jodie, switching off Pia's bedside light. 'Gordon says Sam's told you about your grandmother?'

'About the first baby, and Nan, and Grandad, and then you? Yes.' She'd nodded, wanting to reach across and touch her mother, but somehow knowing that would be wrong.

'Well, you see, your nan never told *me* all that. Maybe if she had it would have made sense. But when I met your dad, I was young, very stupid. It –' she turned back to the girl, 'it all happened again! Full circle, if you like!

'I was pregnant, too. Not with you. And we didn't lose the baby. We' – she'd suddenly buried her face in her hands – 'got rid of it. It was Bob's idea. What he wanted. No one knew. Only Gordon. He wanted to marry me. He wanted to take care of us, me and whatever it would have been. But I was over my head. I thought your father was the only magical thing in the world that would ever make sense to me. You know what I mean?'

Jodie had nodded solemnly, and this time it had been Karen who'd reached across and touched her hand.

'So it was done. Then everything else was arranged. Passports. Emigration forms. Everything. Bob and I were married in Stoke.' Her eyes had clouded, looking somewhere long ago. 'We were ready to leave. I came back here, packed my things, and then I found your nan's diary. I found out all about her and her world, and what I'd been to your grandad and herself.

'I read it all.' Her mother's voice had sounded strangled. 'And I swore, the night I left England for what I was sure would be the last time, that it would never happen again if *I* ever had a daughter.

'I have a daughter.' They'd looked at each other, and Pia had sighed in her sleep. 'I didn't worry about you in Australia. Somehow, on the farm, even in Sydney, you were just a little girl, like Pia.

'Then when we came back, when I found Gordon had a son, when your nan and I discovered you and Sam were seeing each other, we both panicked. Both for exactly the same reason, only we thought it was different, because we'd never talked to each other properly.'

'The way you and I haven't, you mean?' Jodie had blinked back the dustiness of sleep and tried to focus on her mother.

'Yes.' Karen had nodded slowly. 'Nan thought she was protecting me. I thought I was protecting you. We were both wrong.'

'Now?' Despite herself, Jodie had slipped further down under the duvet, cradling it round her, making it into a warm nest.

'I'm sorry. We'll talk. We'll all talk. And Jodie?' This time the hand holding hers had squeezed it firmly. 'Thank you for being you.'

The door had closed softly behind her. The step on the stairs that always creaked had creaked. Then there had been a muttering of voices in the hall, a relaxed, almost-giggle from Karen that Jodie had never heard before – and nothing, until twenty minutes ago when brilliant sunshine, glancing off the white snow, had shaken her awake.

She moved her head and looked towards Pia again.

The little girl slept peacefully, the toy koala cuddled into her neck, her left arm thrown across the covers.

Jodie grinned, basking in the sunlight, then stretched like Edward, got up, padded towards the window, drew back the curtains and looked out at a strange dazzling world where nothing moved and no birds sang.

England. And almost Christmas.

Her smile spread like the sunshine.

At last, it seemed, they were all safe.

CHRISTMAS EVE

The voices of the carol singers in the village dipped and died with the church bells.

Edward woke up, shook his head, scratched his ear with his back paw, then buried both his front ones under his nose.

Barbara Wright threw another log on the fire and smiled to herself.

In another ten minutes Gordon and Karen would come in, stamping snow off their shoes and smiling with all the warmth and embarrassment of any couple who have just decided they could possibly be a couple.

She was glad about that.

Pia grinned up at her as if she'd just read her thoughts, then offered her grandmother a badly burned chestnut.

'It might just taste OK,' she said apologetically, and Barbara, taking it, laughed.

In the window the tree Sam and Gordon had brought five days ago winked and blinked, loaded with golden glitter and shimmering tinsel.

She fussed Edward's head, privately promising him the giblets from the turkey, and even a slice of breast as long as Gordon was doing the carving and Karen could be kept out of the way. Then she looked at the clock, worrying slightly.

Jodie had said she and Sam weren't going to the

midnight service, that they had a service of their own, and that that would be enough.

Barbara guessed they'd take the rose to the stone and bury it under the snow as some kind of token to their own particular gods.

'It's nearly midnight, Nan.' Pia was on her feet, pulling back the curtains at the window by the tree, laughing and jiggling from one foot to the other as if she'd never ever been nearly dead.

'Yes.' She stood up slowly. 'A glass of sherry, I think. And a quarter one for you. Run and get it. There's a good girl.'

Then two voices outside rang across the snow in a kind of imperfect harmony, harking the herald angels and begging Good King Wenceslas to look out.

Barbara looked.

Jodie, carrying a bunch of holly and mistletoe, glanced towards the warmly lit house. Then she smiled at Sam.

'I think it's midnight,' she murmured. 'Happy Christmas.'

A dozen different church bells clamoured from a dozen different villages.

The tree in the window winked its welcome. And something like a shooting star careered across the sky as Sam's arms tightened round her and their lips met.

'Happy Christmas and hello,' he said simply.

'Hello,' she smiled back as the first new flakes of snow licked both their faces.